Michael's Descent:
Four Score and Madness

Anthony DiCristofano

Cover design by Anthony DiCristofano

ISBN: 979-8-9995181-2-5

Table of Contents

Chapter 1: Grates of Wrath

"Fuuuck youuu!" he screamed through the shards of broken glass.

His rage was answered with four more rounds ripping through the door, splinters flying. The bullets missed by inches.

He dropped lower. "That was close."

Sunlight sneaked through the holes in the battered door, dust motes dancing like ghosts in the thin beams. Jagged splinters jutted inward, casting sharp shadows across the cracked floor.

"You motherfuckers!"

"I didn't do ANYTHING!" he yelled, spit flying—rage and fear tangled in his throat like barbed wire.

The door shook again as another volley crashed through. Then, silence.

He crouched lower, breath ragged, muscles drawn tight, coiled like wire. The stench of gunpowder and hot lead thickened the air, clinging to his skin.

Outside, sirens wailed in the distance. Inside, only the sound of his pounding heart and the echo of that cursed name bouncing off the walls of his mind. The fragile thread holding his sanity stretched to the limit.

The gunfire paused.

Now he could hear them, voices murmuring just beyond the walls. Blurred. Angry. Distant.

He listened hard, trying to make sense of the mess. Trying to catch one goddamn word.

What the fuck now?

Surrender? Run? Fight? *Where?*

That relentless motherfucker brought me to this. The thought made his blood boil.

"You son of a bitch!" he screamed.

The reply came in the form of more hot lead, tearing through walls and windows at blistering speed. Glass rained down.

He pressed flat to the floor.

The room closed in.

He had no answers.

Only one question:

What the fuck do I do now?

Chapter 2: The Good Life

Part One: The Mold

Before the alarm. Before the lights, the collar, the clean lines of a normal day. There was this.

Silence.

Not peace, just the dull, ambient hush of a small house in a well-behaved suburb. Outside, the world was still wrapped in early gray, a smear of clouds and trimmed hedges. Inside, the air sat heavy and still, broken only by the soft click of the HVAC and the refrigerator's occasional sigh.

Michael lay awake in bed, staring at the ceiling. He'd been up for twenty-three minutes. The phone alarm hadn't gone off yet. He never let it.

He liked this stretch of time, before decisions, before mirrors, before pretending.

His mother used to call it his "quiet clock." Said he'd always had it. Even as a kid, he'd wake early and just... exist. No noise. No questions. Just lay there, eyes wide, waiting for the day to start like a polite guest at a locked door.

She thought it was sweet.

Later, he'd wonder if it was anxiety.

The house still smelled like lavender dryer sheets and faint lemon floor cleaner, leftover comfort from a life that wasn't entirely his. His mother had passed a few years back, and yet her ghost lived in the cabinet arrangement, the folded towels, the compulsion to make things tidy before sleep.

She had loved him hard. Protected him even harder. Sometimes it felt like she'd padded his world with so much soft fabric he never grew the calluses he needed.

Not like his brother.

Michael rolled onto his side, eyes drifting toward the closet. Inside, his shirts were arranged by shade, light to dark, business casual to client-ready. A choice he made once, and then never questioned again.

It hadn't always been this way. He hadn't always cared about order. That came later—after the father left, after the world felt too big and loud. After Michael realized that being **prepared** was the only way to avoid being **like him**, a man who showed up half-drunk, half-present, and then eventually not at all.

Michael barely remembered his face, just the feeling he left behind, sharp, like cold metal. A presence that didn't hug, didn't praise. Just watched. Judged. Then vanished.

His older brother remembered more. And he wore that memory like armor. Built a life out of it. Out west now, working the lines, wiring mountains, breaking calluses just to keep them sharp. He didn't do ties. Didn't do meetings. Said Michael's life was "safety with a choke collar."

Michael said nothing at the time, but the phrase stuck. Still does.

He pushed the blanket off and sat up, bare feet touching cold wood floor. No hesitation. No ceremony. Just motion. The start of a curated day.

He had made choices, safe ones. Straight-line ones. No sharp turns.
He had a title. A savings account. A lawn service.
He drank filtered water and paid for the version of Spotify that didn't interrupt his thoughts.
He did everything right.

So why, some mornings, did he feel like he was standing on the edge of something old and sharp, something waiting just beneath the veneer?

Why did he sometimes feel like he hadn't escaped his father's gravity at all, just learned how to simulate flight?

The alarm buzzed from the nightstand. 6:35 a.m. He was already standing.

Time to start the day.

Part Two: A Polished Shell

Michael backed out of the driveway with the slow, practiced confidence of someone who knew exactly how much clearance he had on either side. The Range Rover, black, gleaming, still flawless, moved like a shark through the quiet suburb. Its engine hummed a sound of subdued wealth, not opulence. The kind of vehicle that said, *I'm not rich, but I make good decisions.*

He liked that illusion.

Inside the cabin, the smell of Italian leather mixed with faint hints of cologne and last night's drive-thru coffee. The dashboard lit up with soft blue light, every detail curated to suggest control, order, dominance over the day.

He flipped through radio stations. Classical. Too slow. NPR. Too grim. Sports talk. Too loud. Eventually, he settled on a playlist Kayla had made months ago, instrumental background music with names like *Focus Flow* and *Crush It Mode*. It felt artificial now. But everything did, lately.

The drive to the office was smooth, uneventful. Dublin, Ohio, played its role perfectly: clean medians, freshly painted lane lines, school buses making their early runs. Parents walking kids to school, joggers pretending not to check their Apple Watches every three seconds.

Every house seemed a little too well-kept. Every lawn a little too uniform. It was the kind of town where people didn't shout, they filed complaints. Where suffering wasn't visible, it was internalized, manicured, and medicated.

At a red light, he glanced at the Range Rover's console. Heated and cooled seats. Massage function. Voice control. All the bells and whistles. He remembered showing it off to his brother on a rare visit, trying to impress the man who could skin and quarter a deer without flinching but didn't own a single button-down shirt.

"Nice," his brother had grunted, running a hand over the leather, unimpressed. "But can it climb a mountain?"

Michael had laughed then. But it had stung.

Pulling into the office lot, he found his usual spot. He liked to park near the middle, not too close to the door, didn't want to look lazy, but not too far either. Appearances mattered. At least, they used to.

He cut the engine. The quiet that followed was always jarring. He sat for a moment, just breathing, the weight of the day not yet upon him but close enough to cast a shadow.

Part Three: The Morning Game

The elevator's brushed metal doors whispered shut behind him with a gentle sigh. Michael stood alone inside, hands folded in front of him like a man awaiting judgment. He watched the floor numbers tick upward, reflected in the mirrored panels: 3... 4... 5... slow breath... 6... eyes forward... 7.

A quiet bell. A clean slide of doors.

The Client Solutions floor smelled of citrus disinfectant and burnt coffee grounds. A few voices floated through the office, tempered, polite. Laughter that didn't travel past the break room.

Michael moved with the precise rhythm of someone who knew the choreography by heart. His shoes clicked just loud enough to signal presence but not interruption. A nod here, a smile there, Paige from

7

Analytics gave him a too-bright "Morning!" as she stirred something oat-based in a Mason jar.

He nodded back, perfectly dialed. Approachable, but busy.

His workspace was a glass half-wall cubicle with dual monitors, a personalized ergonomic chair, and a small potted succulent that someone once said was "a gift," though he couldn't remember from who. It hadn't died. He took that as a win.

He slid into the chair and tapped the keyboard. The screens blinked awake with dashboards and metrics and a color-coded inbox that scrolled longer than he'd remembered. Twelve flagged emails. Three meetings. One client concern. Five nudges. All framed in cheery corporate urgency.

He responded to one. Closed another. The rest he let hover in the periphery.

His reflection ghosted on the darkened second monitor, faint, muted, professional. The kind of face people trusted in pitch meetings and forgot on lunch breaks.

Behind him, a framed certificate hung at perfect angle: *Q2 Engagement Leader – Michael T.* The printed signature at the bottom belonged to someone who'd been laid off last quarter. He didn't take it down. It filled the wall space and looked good during Zooms.

He pulled out his stainless steel water bottle, one of three identical ones he kept in rotation, and gave it a shake. The protein mix had separated again. It always did. The vanilla clumped like resignation.

He drank anyway. Grimaced. Opened a spreadsheet.

The first meeting of the day blinked on his calendar: "Quick Sync – Client Strat." The subject line was a half-formed question. The invite had no agenda. He accepted it anyway. Declining meant you had feelings. Accepting meant you had a process.

From the far end of the floor, someone laughed too loudly. Probably Greg. Or someone like him. Michael didn't turn to check.

Instead, he stared for a moment at the desktop background, a default stock image of a shoreline at dusk, filtered to a corporate blue-gray. Peaceful. Distant. He'd never bothered changing it.

He leaned back slightly, adjusted his shirt cuffs, and watched the minute hand crawl toward 9:00.

Another day. Another room. Another version of himself.

And all of them smiling.

Part Four: Cruise Control

The sun was low and wide, throwing honey-colored light across the windshields and signage as Michael steered onto the highway ramp with the kind of fluid confidence that came from daily repetition. The Range Rover slid into the middle lane like it belonged there, like he belonged there.

The city peeled away behind him in soft gradients: glass to concrete to chain-link to sprawl. Dublin was only twenty-five minutes from the office with no traffic, and he knew every merge, every sign, every slowdown. This stretch was usually smooth.

But not today.

About five miles in, brake lights bloomed ahead like a field of dying embers. A sea of red. One after another, cars slowed, then stopped. Michael tapped the brakes, adjusted his posture, and sighed, quietly, controlled.

He flicked on his turn signal, eased into the right lane, and crept forward at a crawl. Every few yards, another car cut in ahead. No one waved. No one merged with grace. The lane closures had turned into silent, asphalt warfare.

His thumb tapped the steering wheel like it could will the cars ahead to disappear.

He inched forward, watching the skyline shrink in the rearview mirror. He turned down the volume on the background playlist Kayla had made, he couldn't stand the synthetic optimism of "Crush It Mode" while stuck behind a minivan with a "Baby on Board" sticker and a tail light held on with duct tape.

A few cars up, an SUV refused to let a sedan merge. Horns. Hands. A mild stand-off. Michael gritted his teeth.

It took twenty minutes to crawl a mile.

He adjusted the AC. Then again. Too cold. Too loud. He turned it off. Rolled down the window. The hot air hit him like a hair dryer dipped in exhaust fumes. He rolled it back up.

When he finally reached the bottleneck, he leaned slightly forward, eyes narrowing.

There it was.

Some beat-up sedan, late nineties, maybe a Saturn or a Civic, sat dead in the far lane with its hazard lights weakly blinking. The hood was up, and beneath it, a man moved like a boxer too deep into the twelfth round. Shirt soaked through, arms black with grime, a rag tossed uselessly on the engine block.

The guy looked early forties, maybe younger if you scraped off the miles. His whole body screamed heat, frustration, and some kind of desperation Michael didn't want to name.

"Freaking loser," he muttered under his breath, just loud enough to count.

He didn't look the man in the eye as he passed, but he didn't look away either. Just a side-glance. A quick inventory of failure. No road flares. No AAA sticker. Just a man sweating into a machine that didn't care.

Michael kept his foot light on the gas. Merged. Moved on.

But the image lingered.

The guy's open hood. The useless rag. The look of someone who'd had too many things go wrong for one day.

Michael rolled his shoulders, stretched his neck, tried to shake the weight that had settled at the base of his skull. That wouldn't be him. Couldn't be. He made good choices. He planned. He changed his oil every six thousand miles and never let his gas tank drop below a quarter. He had a maintenance schedule. A premium service account. Extended warranty.

That guy was someone else's cautionary tale.

He flicked on his blinker and veered off at the next exit without thinking. Just something about the heat. The traffic. The idea of home felt suffocating now, like walking straight from gridlock into a glass box of silence.

Whole Foods appeared just off the frontage road, tucked between a boutique dog spa and an upscale nail bar.

He flicked on his turn signal and veered into the lot.

Part Five: Aspirational Grocery

Inside Whole Foods, the air smelled like eucalyptus and inflated self-worth. Everything had a label, organic, sustainable, humanely raised, locally sourced, imported, gluten-free but spiritually nourishing. Michael moved through the aisles with practiced grace, eyes scanning without urgency.

He didn't need much. But he didn't need a reason, either.

He picked up a carton of oat milk he didn't like but kept buying, because Kayla once said it was better for the planet. He grabbed a small bag of heirloom cherry tomatoes, one avocado, a shrink-wrapped packet of pre-cooked wild rice, and an artisanal hot sauce that cost more than his first week's groceries in college.

None of it would make a meal. But it looked like intention.

The checkout line was quiet. A cashier with half her head shaved and a nose ring scanned his items like she was judging their carbon footprint. Michael smiled politely. She didn't smile back.

He tapped his card. Declined. Tried again. Approved.

As he walked out, a man in joggers and a Patagonia vest brushed past him holding a twelve-pack of electrolyte water and three kombucha bottles. The man's eyes never met his.

Back in the car, Michael set the groceries gently in the passenger seat like they might bruise from sudden movement. The dashboard clock glowed 6:11 p.m.

He sat there a moment, watching the sky shift pink, then turned the engine and slid back into traffic.

Part Six: The Circle

The neighborhood curled inward like a gated secret, a cul-de-sac designed for quiet desperation and moderate success. The kind of street where people still waved but didn't really want to talk. Michael turned in slowly, Range Rover humming like a well-fed housecat.

He kept the music low. Not off, just low enough to suggest he enjoyed ambience, not noise.

To his left, the Baker kids were back in the yard again. Sidewalk chalk in a loose spray across the concrete, one kid shirtless and holding a garden hose like a bazooka. The dad, Greg or Craig or something equally underwhelming, stood in the driveway holding a beer he probably didn't earn, watching his offspring run feral with an expression of bland approval.

Michael resisted the urge to sigh. Loudly.

"Classy," he muttered under his breath, easing past them at an even twelve miles per hour. "Nothing says generational success like warm Miller Lite and weaponized toddlers."

Next door, an aging Craftsman-style house had a hedge growing just enough to suggest surrender. The porch light was on, even though it wasn't dark yet. Michael made a mental note, again, that the brick mailbox was still slightly crooked after three months. Probably one of those families that said things like "we'll get to it" while watching their siding rot from the inside.

Across the street, a retired couple stood at their mailbox in matching windbreakers, pretending not to notice him. The woman gave a smile that didn't quite reach her eyes. Michael returned it with corporate precision: two seconds of upward curve, no teeth, a nod timed for maximum blandness.

The Range Rover glided into his own driveway with perfect alignment, front wheels settled just short of the garage like choreography. He turned off the ignition and sat for a moment, watching the house settle into frame like a photograph.

It was clean. It was quiet. It was his.

He opened the door and stepped out. The air was cool now, touched with that early evening scent of fresh-cut grass and something faintly artificial, dryer sheets maybe, or whatever the Bakers used to fumigate their yard.

He paused for a beat, hands on his hips, surveying his domain.

This was order. This was what success looked like when it wasn't showing off.

Inside, the house waited, still, curated, a reflection of the man who lived in it.

Or at least, the man he was supposed to be.

Part Seven: Dinner with Kayla

She arrived in the way she always did, unannounced but expected, dressed like a Pinterest board had sneezed on her. Kayla glided in through the front door with the soft rustle of synthetic fabric, her oversized glasses slipping slightly down the bridge of her nose as she gave Michael a once-over that wasn't quite a compliment.

"Heyyy," she said, drawing it out like a greeting and a sigh.

"Hey," he replied, already moving toward the kitchen, already thinking about the wine.

She wandered through the living room, phone in hand, thumbs already scrolling as she sank into the neutral-toned sectional he'd picked for its showroom appeal. Her legs curled up underneath her like a practiced influencer pose. Her phone reflected back in her lenses, rings of blue light flickering across glass she didn't need.

Michael glanced over as he uncorked the bottle.

"When did you start wearing glasses?" he asked.

She didn't look up. "Oh, like a couple months ago? They're fake. It's just a look."

He poured the wine. Deep red, from a bottle that cost enough to imply intention. He held both glasses for a moment, waiting to see if she'd glance up. She didn't.

"Here," he said, walking it over.

She took the glass absently, eyes still on her phone, then blinked and smiled like she remembered she was supposed to.

"Oh my God, thank you," she said, and kissed the air near his cheek. "You're like... the best."

They sat for a moment with the easy silence of people who had stopped asking real questions a while ago. Kayla scrolled. Michael sipped.

Dinner was roasted salmon, wild rice, and vegetables he'd sautéed just right. He had plated everything cleanly, like a lifestyle blog post in progress. She didn't notice the plating, but she said "This is really good" between bites, so he took that as a win.

She talked mostly about people he didn't know, someone from yoga who got dumped, a girl from her building who just got a collab offer from a sustainable leggings brand. He nodded in the right places. Smiled where it counted. Her sentences were dotted with phrases like "super cute," "kinda toxic," and "you should've seen it."

He kept his responses brief and agreeable.

At one point, she laughed at something on her phone. Loud. Startling.

"What?" he asked.

She turned the screen toward him for a second, but it was too fast to read. A meme. A reel. A guy dancing in a banana costume or a chihuahua in sunglasses. He gave a polite half-laugh. She grinned and went back to scrolling.

After dinner, they drifted to the couch. She curled up next to him but didn't put her phone down. Her head rested lightly on his shoulder. He stayed very still, not wanting to ruin it.

The expensive wine sat half-finished on the coffee table.

Later, she fell asleep halfway through an episode of something neither of them were really watching. He muted the TV and stared at the ceiling.

For a moment, he let himself imagine this as stability. As connection. As enough.

Maybe this was it. Maybe this was what adulthood looked like, something close enough to happiness that you stopped questioning it.

He reached for the remote and turned the screen black.

In the dark, her phone buzzed again—twice, then stopped.

Michael didn't look at it. He just sat there, eyes open, letting the silence settle.

Part Eight: Just Another Morning

The alarm buzzed at 6:35 a.m. sharp, right on cue, gentle, polite, one of those tones designed to suggest mindfulness instead of urgency.

Michael silenced it with a practiced tap, then let his hand drift back down to the sheets. Beside him, Kayla stirred slightly, her breath slow and warm against his shoulder.

The bedroom was dim, shaded by blackout curtains that still couldn't keep the early morning entirely out. A sliver of sunlight peeked through one corner, painting a golden line across the far wall.

He didn't move. Not yet.

Kayla's leg was draped across his. Her hair, wild and sun-touched, fanned out against the pillow like a commercial for sleep he could never quite achieve. She smelled like lavender and the fancy shampoo she always said was too expensive but bought anyway.

For once, she wasn't scrolling. Just sleeping.

Michael stared at the ceiling and let himself feel good. Not ecstatic, not euphoric, just... settled. The air was cool, the sheets soft, the house still.

Everything felt balanced.

Later, they'd have coffee. He'd make her eggs. She'd sit at the counter in one of his old T-shirts and tell him about a dream she had or a skincare trend she saw. He'd pretend to be interested, and maybe he wouldn't have to pretend that hard.

It was Thursday. He had meetings, but nothing heavy. A few calls. A strategy session that might get pushed. He thought about wearing the navy shirt today—the one that made his shoulders look better on Zoom.

He didn't feel dread. He didn't feel behind. He felt... fine.

He closed his eyes again, just for a second, breathing in the scent of her, the sheets, the faint clean citrus of the diffuser in the hallway.

There was a peace in this. A rhythm. A life that, for all its polish and predictability, had found a kind of quiet joy.

Outside, the neighborhood was still asleep.

Inside, everything was working.

Chapter 3: The Layoff

Part One: Untethered

It started like any other Thursday.

The sun came through the slats of the blinds at just the right angle to catch the brushed steel of Michael's kitchen faucet. His coffee machine hissed its familiar final gasp, and the air smelled like productivity and mild ambition. He shaved carefully that morning. Not rushed, not lazy, deliberate. One of those rare days where his shirt fit right, his collar sat perfectly, and his shoes had just enough polish to reflect the recessed lighting in the hallway.

The drive to the office was smooth. Traffic obeyed him. He found the perfect parking spot, not too close to seem entitled, not too far to break a sweat.

Inside, the building buzzed with its usual low-grade hum of optimism. People smiled. The air smelled faintly of fresh carpet cleaner and cinnamon oatmeal. Someone in HR had brought in donuts. Even Janet, who never brought anything, brought donuts. A little sign was taped to the break room table: "You're the Glaze That Holds Us Together!"

Michael chuckled to himself. He took a maple long john and walked to his desk.

Emails were normal. Slack channels lit up with the usual nonsense, cat GIFs, project delays, minor triumphs. His manager even stopped by and complimented last week's report.

And when the all-hands meeting was announced at 10:45, nobody blinked. Just another one of those team-building, town-hall, alignment-synergy bits the company liked to do once a quarter.

They gathered in the large conference room. Too many people for the number of chairs. A few leaned against the walls. Phones in pockets. Laptops snapped shut.

The CEO didn't even bother showing up. Just a big screen, grainy Zoom feed, corporate backdrop with a city skyline blurred behind the logo.

A woman from the acquisition team began speaking. Calmly. Too calmly.

"…We're excited to announce a partnership that will position us for long-term growth and greater shareholder value."

The words washed over them in abstract waves: **Merger. Strategic Alignment. Brand Integration. Transition of Key Functions.**

Then came the phrase no one mistook for anything else:

"Lincoln Talon Acquisitions."

Michael sat up straighter.

The same Lincoln Talon Acquisitions they'd once joked about, too big, too slow, too "old man." The company that ate smaller firms like a python swallowing rabbits. Slowly. Whole.

He felt it in his gut first. A tightening.

The meeting continued. Smiles froze. Heads tilted.

And then came the final blow, dropped with the casual cruelty only upper management could master:

"…and unfortunately, as part of this integration, several positions will be made redundant effective today…"

Silence. Not gasps. Not cries. Just that perfect corporate stillness. Like a church with fluorescent lighting.

Angela from HR reappeared in his doorway less than fifteen minutes later.

"Michael, can I grab you for just a second?"

The walk down the hallway felt different now. Like a funeral procession where only one person knew they were the body.

This time, he noticed how quiet everything had become. People glanced sideways. Not directly at him — just near him. Like something might rub off.

He entered the glass conference room.

Angela smiled gently. A legal rep. A new face from "Transition Support."

The folder was already waiting. Severance. Thirty days of benefits. Career coaching. Resume workshops.

And a mug. White ceramic with the company logo and "Michael T." printed in dull silver across the front.

Inside the mug was a rolled-up mousepad. Branded with a motivational slogan so generic it felt like a slap: **"Innovate. Integrate. Inspire."**

A box appeared beside it. Neatly packed. His personal effects: pens, a photo of Kayla, his reusable water bottle, the framed quote from his mother he kept behind his monitor.

Angela said words, soft, practiced, noncommittal. Something about "appreciation for his years" and "exciting opportunities ahead."

He didn't hear them. Not really.

He stood slowly. Picked up the box.

Angela stood too, as did the others. No one shook his hand.

As he turned to leave, the weight of the cardboard dug into his palms. Not heavy, but humiliating. Every item inside a tiny echo of the years he'd given away.

The hallway had changed again.

It was still quiet, but now it was pretending not to be. The low hum of keyboards felt staged. Conversations stalled as he passed.

No one looked directly at him. No one waved.

He reached the elevator. Pressed the button.

Waited.

Waited.

When the doors opened, he stepped in alone. The box hugged to his chest like a child clutching a pillow in the dark.

The ride down felt slow.

Lobby music played from a speaker above, something cheerful, forgettable, soul-warping in its indifference.

When the doors slid open, the receptionist gave him a half-nod without breaking eye contact from her screen.

Outside, the sunlight was too bright.

The walk to his car took longer than he remembered. Each step landing slightly out of rhythm, like he was walking in a body that didn't quite fit anymore.

He unlocked the door, set the box in the passenger seat, and sat in the driver's side with the engine off.

His hands rested on the steering wheel. Still. Tight.

He stared out through the windshield.

From this angle, the building looked clean, professional, proud.

Like nothing had happened.

Part Two: The Drive Home

The seatbelt clicked with a finality that felt personal. Michael turned the key. The Range Rover hummed to life with its usual quiet purr, oblivious to the shift in status inside its cabin.

He pulled out of the lot without looking back.

The silence inside the vehicle was deafening. No radio. No podcasts. Just the sound of tires gliding across the corporate asphalt and the low whistle of the air conditioning. The box on the passenger seat rattled slightly as he made a left out of the complex, his name still scrawled in marker across the lid like a posthumous signature.

His jaw clenched. His left hand tapped the steering wheel, not from rhythm but from kinetic rage, contained, for now.

He stared ahead, jaw tight, trying to focus on the road, on the feel of control, tires gripping pavement, turn signals blinking with certainty, the car still obeying his commands even if nothing else did.

"Eight years," he said out loud. To no one. "Eight years and I get a mug."

The dashboard blinked. A soft blue notification: **"Reminder: 5:00 PM - Wine with Kayla."**
He snorted. "Still on the calendar. How sweet."

This is just a bump. He'd bounce back. He had options. He had some savings. He had a Range Rover.

His fingers gripped the wheel tighter.

"I'm fine," he said aloud. "I'm good."

He took the next exit. The traffic thinned. The world calmed.

Dublin looked the same. Too green. Too pleasant. Too clean.

He passed rows of planned homes and carefully constructed smiles, HOA-approved color palettes and kids on scooters.

His phone buzzed.

Kayla: **"See you soon 🌚"**

He stared at the message. No response. Not yet.

The sun dipped lower. Shadows stretched across the pavement. He turned onto his street, each familiar mailbox standing like a smug witness.

He pulled into the driveway slowly, Range Rover gliding to its final stop like a prize show dog returning from competition.

He sat there a moment before turning off the ignition.

His reflection hovered faintly in the windshield, neat shirt, still pressed, face still calm. On the surface, nothing had changed.

He reached over and touched the box. The mug inside clinked softly.

Part Three: The Box on the Counter

Evening. The light is low and indifferent. The kitchen feels larger when hope is missing.

Michael sat at the counter, elbows on the cool granite, staring at the cardboard box like it might blink. It had been there for hours — right where he set it after getting home. Inside: his stapler, the framed photo of him and Kayla at the zoo, the mug, the mousepad. The mug still had a Post-it stuck inside. *You'll be missed!*

He hadn't touched the box since. Didn't have the strength.

The door opened with its usual click, the sound of presence entering a space that no longer felt private. He didn't move.

"Hey babe," Kayla's voice floated in, all sunshine and casual breathiness. The same tone she used to greet her barista. Her boots clacked lightly on the hardwood. She dropped her oversized bag near the door like she lived here, even though she didn't.

Michael didn't answer right away. Just stared at the mug inside the box. The silence stretched.

She rounded the corner into the kitchen, her phone already in hand. Those enormous round-frame glasses perched on her nose, part owl, part influencer. She was wearing a loose cardigan over a tank top, casual effort, like a curated lifestyle post.

Her gaze landed on the box.

She slowed. Blinked. "What's this?"

He didn't turn. "They laid me off."

A pause. Just long enough to be noticeable. "Oh."

That was it. One syllable. Not *what happened?*, not *are you okay?*, not even *Jesus, seriously?*

Just *oh*, like she'd forgotten to charge her phone overnight. Like he'd spilled something.

She stepped a little closer, glanced at the box again, then picked up the wine bottle he'd laid out earlier, a nice Syrah, not cheap. She didn't comment. Just turned it in her hand like she was scanning for the label aesthetic.

Michael finally looked up. Her eyes weren't on him. They were on her reflection in the microwave door.

The quiet swelled between them.

He didn't want to explain. Didn't want to say how it happened or what it meant. He just wanted to know what she'd do. But she did nothing. No hand on his shoulder. No sitting down next to him. No surprise. Just that little tight-lipped expression that meant she was calculating.

She set the bottle down. "Do you still want to open this?"

He hesitated. Then: "Sure."

The word sounded like someone else said it.

She walked to the drawer for the corkscrew. He watched her, feeling something shift, slow, seismic. Like noticing the tide had gone out and taken something vital with it.

Later that night, after she left, he lay on the couch, staring into the ceiling's blankness. Her scent lingered faintly, floral and synthetic. His phone lit up once, a short text.

"Thanks for dinner. xo"

No emojis. No "love you." Just polite efficiency.

He turned the screen over and closed his eyes.

For a moment, he let himself imagine this as stability. As connection. As enough.

But the silence disagreed.

Chapter 4: The Descent Begins

The cork didn't so much *pop* as it surrendered. A limp little sigh escaped the cheap bottle as Michael twisted it free, the label already peeling slightly from the humidity near the sink.

He stared at the wine for a moment, tilting the bottle as if the color might redeem it, but it looked watery, thin. It was the kind of wine that didn't get uncorked so much as tolerated.

He poured it anyway.

In the background, the pan sizzled softly. Dinner was already simmering, a one-pan deal, mostly canned ingredients. He had convinced himself it was still decent. Rustic, maybe. Earthy. Whatever word people used when they meant *cheap but edible*.

He heard the front door open, no knock, just the usual shuffle of Kayla's boots on the welcome mat.

"Hey," he called, not turning. "Just about ready."

"Hey," she answered, her voice flat, already halfway distracted.

He heard the familiar sound of her phone being set on the counter, followed by the faint tapping of her thumbs, still texting, still scrolling.

She drifted into the kitchen without much of a glance at the stove or the man manning it.

"What is that?" she asked, nodding toward the wineglass.

Michael didn't turn. "Cabernet. Sort of."

He stirred the pan slowly, pretending not to hear the subtext. "Didn't feel like dropping twenty bucks on a bottle this week."

Kayla didn't respond.

She pulled out a chair and sat with a slow, performative sigh, sliding her phone onto the table where it continued to light up every few seconds. Notifications. Always something more interesting than this.

Michael plated the food, steaming, humble, and set one dish in front of her. He didn't expect a compliment, but some acknowledgment would've been nice.

She poked at it with her fork. "Is this... quinoa?"

"Barley," he said. "It's what I had."

She gave a tight, unimpressed smile. "Right. Very... wholesome."

They ate in silence for a few minutes, the only sounds the clink of fork on ceramic and the occasional buzz of her phone.

He watched her across the table. Her oversized glasses caught the light, reflecting back the faint glow of her screen more than her eyes.

"You've been busy lately," he said, casually, or tried to.

She shrugged. "Work's been crazy. And my mom's been texting me about this trip we might do, so... yeah."

He nodded. "You mentioned that."

She didn't ask about his job hunt. Or how his day was. Or anything, really.

She took another half-hearted bite of food, then reached for her phone again.

Michael looked down at his plate. He wasn't hungry anymore.

The dishes clinked dully in the sink. Neither of them moved to clean up. The bottle sat half-empty on the table, the cheap label peeling slightly.

Kayla scrolled her phone, thumb moving with mechanical precision. Her plate still had food on it, pushed into a lazy crescent like she'd rearranged it to feign interest. Michael sat across from her, eyes heavy, fork in hand but unmoving.

"You okay?" he asked quietly.

She didn't look up. "Mmhmm."

The silence crept in like a draft. Michael swallowed, his throat dry. He reached for his glass, took a sip of the wine, and winced slightly. Flat. Acidic. Cheap.

Kayla finally glanced up. "This is different."

He blinked. "What?"

"The wine," she said, raising her glass and giving it a little swirl. "It's not the usual."

He nodded. "Yeah. It was... on sale."

Her brow lifted just slightly, a flicker of something, judgment, or maybe disappointment, crossing her face before she buried it again behind the glass.

He watched her drink. Watched the way she didn't comment further. Didn't smile. Didn't reach across the table like she used to. Just drank, then looked at her phone again.

He let the silence stretch. He couldn't bring himself to fill it.

After a few more minutes of quiet chewing and scrolling, she finally broke it, not with warmth, but with a gentle, clinical sort of detachment.

"I feel like we should talk soon," she said, not looking at him.

Michael's eyes flicked to her face. "About what?"

"I don't know." She shrugged. "Just… things. Us."

He gave a small nod. That was all he could manage.

For a moment, neither of them spoke. The hum of the refrigerator filled the room. Outside, the streetlights buzzed in the humid air.

Then she stood up, slowly, gathering her phone and her purse.

"I'm gonna head out. Got an early thing tomorrow."

"Sure," he said, standing too quickly, the legs of his chair scraping the tile. "I'll walk you out."

She hesitated, then smiled — not warmly, but politely. Like a cashier might. "You don't have to."

But he did.

At the door, she gave him a quick peck on the cheek. No eye contact. No linger. Just a motion. A habit.

Then she left.

Michael stood in the doorway a moment longer, watching her taillights dissolve into the dark.

Moths swarmed the golden glow of the porch light, frantic and aimless.

He stepped back inside.

With a soft click, he shut off the light.

The bulb dimmed, faded, and as the gold retreated, the moths scattered, vanishing into the cool night air.

He turned back toward the table. The empty plate. The bottle of discount wine. The two glasses, only one of them drained.

Chapter 5: The Breakup

It wasn't even dark out.

Michael hadn't expected her. She hadn't texted. Just showed up, unannounced, unhurried, like someone stopping by to return a borrowed jacket.

He opened the door, and there she was, standing with her arms folded and her expression unreadable.

"Hey," she said.

"Hey," he answered, stepping aside. "Come in."

She didn't kiss him. Didn't smile. She walked past him into the house like she didn't live in the moment anymore, like she was already somewhere else.

She stood in the middle of the living room, looking around like she hadn't been there before. Her eyes skimmed the bookshelf, the couch, the half-wilted plant in the corner. A beat of silence stretched between them.

Michael waited. She didn't sit.

"You want water or something?" he asked, already knowing the answer.

"No, I'm fine."

He nodded and crossed his arms. "So… what's up?"

She paused, just long enough to make it awkward. "We should talk."

His stomach dropped. The words weren't loud, but they carried a finality he recognized instantly.

He laughed once, short and dry. "Right. That kind of talk."

Kayla didn't flinch. "I don't think this is working."

He looked at her for a long second. "You don't think *what's* working?"

"This," she said, gesturing vaguely between them. "Us. I don't know… it just doesn't feel the same anymore."

"Because I lost my job."

"No," she said quickly. Too quickly. "That's not it."

He tilted his head. "Really?"

A flicker of guilt crossed her face, the first emotion she'd shown since walking in. "I mean… yeah, maybe that's part of it. But it's not about the money. It's about… fulfillment. About where we're going. I don't feel—" she faltered for a moment "—connected. Anymore."

He stared at her, then at the floor, then back at her.

"Are you seeing someone?"

She didn't answer right away.

His eyes narrowed. "Kayla."

She sighed, then met his gaze. "It's… someone I reconnected with. You remember Bobby Lincoln?"

He blinked. The name hit like a slap.

"That ugly fuck?" The words shot out before he could filter them. "That rich little sh*t who had everything handed to him? Are you kidding me?"

Kayla stiffened. "Jesus, Michael. What's wrong with you?"

"What's wrong with *me*?" He laughed, sharp and bitter. "He never worked a day in his life. His dad probably bought his SAT score. That guy was a walking neck-pimple with a trust fund."

"He's actually a great guy," she snapped. "He listens to me. He's *present*. He doesn't act like he's always about to implode."

"Oh, fuck that." Michael's voice cracked, rising with heat. "Of all the people in the world— you pick *him*? Bobby *fucking* Lincoln? Have you no standards left at all?"

Kayla stood, jaw clenched. "You know what, Michael? I didn't come here to get insulted."

"No, you came here to drop a bomb and pretend it's a heart-to-heart. Bravo."

She grabbed her purse. "Enjoy your pity party. I'm done."

The door slammed harder than it needed to, the sound echoing through the small house like a final gavel.

Michael stood frozen, breathing hard, the cheap wine now warm in his glass, untouched.

Outside, her taillights flared, then vanished into the quiet street.

He didn't follow.

He didn't need to.

Bobby fucking Lincoln....

Chapter 6: The Attrition's Scalpel

Michael's mailbox was an unholy archive, a slow-motion execution piled in envelopes, each one heavier than the last.

The first notice had arrived weeks ago, tucked between a catalog and a credit card offer he never opened. It had a quiet, almost polite tone: *"Your payment is past due."*

He threw it on the kitchen counter like a shrug.

The second notice was bolder, a thick envelope, red-inked stamps screaming: *"Final Warning: Immediate Action Required."*

This time, he felt a prickle of panic, but still tried to convince himself it was a clerical error, or a temporary glitch in a life that had been on autopilot too long.

Then came the third: a certified letter that smelled of ink and government offices, *"Repossession proceedings will commence if payment is not received within 7 days."*

Michael sat at the small kitchen table, the same table where he and Kayla had toasted last year with expensive wine, eating prime rib and laughing about nothing.

Now, the table held only a stack of bills, unopened letters, and a half-empty bottle of cheap whiskey.

He held the latest letter in his hand, the paper rough and biting like a slap. Outside, the late afternoon sun splintered through the blinds, casting bars of light and shadow across the envelope, as if his fate was being sentenced right there in his kitchen. They don't come with guns anymore," Michael thought. "Just scalpels. Paper scalpels. Quiet cuts from men in suits."

His Range Rover sat outside, parked crookedly on the driveway, the gleaming machine that had once been the crown jewel of his life now a glaring symbol of everything slipping away.

The chrome reflected the dying sun like a fading halo.

He thought about the first time he slid into those leather seats — the soft, intoxicating smell of new car, the way the steering wheel felt like an extension of his hand, the power under his foot like a secret no one else could have.

The realization clawed at him: this beast was not his anymore. It was a beast with a leash, and the leash was getting shorter by the day.

He put down the letter and ran his fingers through his hair, jaw tight.

The mail continued to come, each envelope a new shard tearing away at his pride.

He opened another today, a bright yellow sticker inside that he knew would soon appear on the windshield, *"Repossession Notice: Final Warning."*

He pictured it already stuck there, mocking him in broad daylight.

Michael pressed the letter against his chest, the paper crumpling slightly.

A ritual now, gathering pieces of himself that were falling apart.

The kitchen clock ticked loudly, indifferent.

Outside, the Range Rover's glossy surface shimmered in the dying light, a fragile monument to better days, and the impending end of them.

Chapter 7: The Repossession

The morning sun slipped through the blinds, soft gold fingers reaching across the bathroom tiles.
Michael stood under the spray of the shower, water running warm against his skin, trying to wash away the weight pressing on his chest.

Then — *thud. Thud. Thud.*

A noise, sharp and insistent, from outside. He paused, letting the water hit his face.

Thud. Thud.

Again, louder. Closer. A low rumble rolled past the window.

He stepped out of the spray, wrapped a towel around his waist, and moved toward the kitchen window.

Outside, the street was full of faces he recognized but never wanted to see.

There, parked in the driveway, was the tow truck, bright orange, a snarling beast with a hook and chains that gleamed in the sunlight.

Two men stood by the Range Rover, rough hands, cheap boots, and eyes that didn't care about titles or histories.

The neighbors, the same ones Michael had once looked down on, lined the sidewalks. Some crossed their arms. Others whispered. Their eyes sharp. Judgmental.

Michael's throat went dry. He cinched the towel tighter, his heart pounding a frantic rhythm.

He opened the door, the hinges groaning like a warning.

"Hey! What the hell do you think you're doing?" His voice cracked.

One of the repo men didn't even look up.

"Sir, this is a legal repossession. Your payments are behind."

Michael stepped forward, the last shred of his old confidence flickering.

"I was gonna, I mean, I just need more time."

The other repo man smirked, wiping grease from his hands.

"Yeah, right. Time's up, man. This isn't charity."

The first guy spoke up, not unkindly, just bored. "We're out of Cincinnati. Lincoln Recovery Group. You'll get a full itemization in the mail."

He pulled a clipboard from the side panel and handed Michael a folded carbon-copy slip.

Michael took it without looking, eyes fixed on the tow cable tightening around his Range Rover's front axle.

The former Client Solutions Specialist now stood half-naked, being treated like a vagrant tossed out of an alleyway.

The first repo man shrugged.

"Maybe next time pay your bills, ha ha ha."

Chains rattled as they hooked the Range Rover. The engine gave one last defiant growl... then fell silent.

With each inch the vehicle rose, Michael's heart sank lower.

He stood frozen, watching his last luxury dragged away, the world turning slower, heavier.

The neighbors murmured, some shaking their heads, others smirking. He felt their silent verdicts like punches.

He wanted to scream. To run. To disappear.

But all he did was stand there.

The men climbed into the cab and slammed the doors with grim finality.

The tow truck's engine roared to life, coughing black smoke as it rolled down the street — a low, growling reveille for the neighbors still watching from behind curtains and doorframes, savoring the spectacle.

Michael remained at the edge of the driveway, towel still damp, eyes hollow.

The Range Rover turned the corner and disappeared.

The truck's engine faded into silence, leaving behind nothing but cracked pavement… and a hollow ache.

Michael stood in the driveway long after the tow truck disappeared.

The neighbors began to trickle back inside, slowly, like theatergoers exiting a matinee that didn't live up to the trailer. No one said anything. They didn't have to. Their eyes had done the talking. Judgment baked into every glance, every smirk.

He watched a curtain twitch across the street. Watched a screen door groan shut. Listened to the world resume like nothing had happened.

His towel had slipped a little, but he didn't adjust it.

He just stood there.

The Range Rover was gone. His driveway looked naked without it, exposed. A patch of oil marked where it had rested, like a tombstone without a name.

Michael turned slowly and walked back inside, bare feet slapping against the tile.

The house was too quiet, but not in the peaceful way. Quiet like a vacuum, like everything good had been sucked out of the air and what remained was stale and hollow.

He passed the kitchen table without looking at it, that battlefield of unopened envelopes and passive-aggressive letters printed in red ink. He didn't need to see them again. He'd memorized their tone. Polite. Stern. Then cruel.

In the mirror by the front hallway, he caught his reflection, wet hair, pale skin, the towel still wrapped around him like a half-forgotten excuse.

He looked… blank. Not even angry. Just… erased.

The house echoed. No Kayla. No dog. No background music. No faint click of wine glasses in the sink. Just that silence, and the low hum of the refrigerator pretending everything was still normal.

He walked to the living room and sat on the couch, the towel leaving a damp imprint beneath him. Stared at the blank TV screen. Reached for the remote. Thought better of it. Put it back down.

After a while, he lay back.

The ceiling above him hadn't changed. Still off-white. Still slightly cracked in the corner. Still dumb and uncaring. But now it felt… heavier. Like it was leaning in.

His arms fell to his sides, limp. His chest rose and fell slowly, like his body was deciding whether or not to keep going.

The longer he lay there, the more he could feel the weight of everything.
The towel. The silence. The oil stain in the driveway.
The version of himself that no longer existed.

He closed his eyes.

Not to sleep.

Just to stop seeing.

Chapter 8: Budgeting for Mobility

The house was dim now, late afternoon sun spilling through the blinds in soft, slanted bands.
Michael sat at the kitchen table, hunched, elbows on the Formica, surrounded by unopened envelopes, crumpled notices, and half-drunk glasses of water gone warm.

In front of him: a legal pad with fading blue lines, a dull pencil, and a quiet reckoning.

He wasn't counting every penny he had left, no, that would be too cruel. This was different.

This was the *car budget*.

The absolute maximum he could spend on a vehicle right now without wiping out the last threads of his precarious balance.

He wrote down the number carefully. Repeated it in his head.

$1,200.

A hard ceiling. No wiggle room.

He leaned back in the chair and let out a long breath through his nose. No Range Rovers. No certified pre-owned anything. Hell, even Craigslist felt like a gamble.

He opened his phone, pulled up a browser, and typed without much hope:
Used cars under $1,500 near me.

The screen flickered to life with blurry thumbnails of rust, desperation, and regret.

He scrolled. Pickup trucks with peeling paint and cracked windshields. A Buick with "slight transmission issue." A Hyundai whose hood wouldn't close. An '02 Impala with 263,000 miles and a proud declaration: *"Cold A/C!!"*

Michael closed the tab.

He sat still for a moment longer, pencil tapping the table in a slow, syncopated rhythm.

Then he stood.
Went to the closet.
Stuffed the sock-drawer cash into his wallet like it was Monopoly money.

He didn't say anything. Didn't sigh. Didn't think. Just moved.

The door creaked open, then shut behind him. The sunlight outside hit harder than it should've.

Chapter 9: The Bus Ride to Reality - Chariot to Hell

Michael's hand closed around the overhead strap, sticky and slick beneath his fingers, as if coated in some forgotten residue from the city's endless neglect. The bus lurched forward with a jerk, and a slow wave of unidentifiable liquid sloshed along the rubber floor's deep grooves, a grim tide pulling back and forth with the vehicle's uneven breath—accelerate, brake, accelerate, brake—like the heartbeat of a broken machine.

Around him, the thin seat cushions sagged and frayed, cloth worn thin to threadbare, mottled with hardened clumps of chewing gum and patches that whispered of stains no one dared name. The sour, sharp smell of stale urine and rotting puke settled in the air, weaving with the metallic clangs and the occasional hiss of the brakes, wrapping the passengers in a blanket of decay.

Across from him, a man sat with eyes fixed, unyielding, unblinking. His gaze felt like it cut through Michael's skin, burning slow trails into the flesh beneath. The man muttered inaudible words, a restless murmur barely lost in the murmuring engine, but heavy in the silence of shared misery.

Behind Michael, the cough came again, dry, ragged, relentless, each hack a spatter of sound pounding against the back of his head, a metronome marking time in the unsteady symphony of despair.

Nearby, the homeless man was a shifting mass of tattered fabric, four pairs of pants, layered sweaters, patchwork armor against a world that didn't care. His feet, blackened and cracked, were cradled in his hands as he rubbed them obsessively, shedding thin curls of skin that floated down like strange, pale leaves drifting through the stale air.

Somewhere in the middle of the bus, a man leaned too close to a young woman, his breath heavy with cheap whiskey and something fouled by desperation. She glanced away, eyes wide and frightened, the unspoken tension thick as smoke in the cramped space.

At the front, a storm broke loose, a passenger erupting in curses, threats to yank the driver out by her collar. The driver's calm, clipped replies barely cut through the shouting, but the chaos spiraled through the bus, a wild pulse beating against the thin walls.

Michael blinked slowly, his throat dry. He thought of the Range Rover, its leather seats cool and smooth, the hum of the engine like a promise whispered in silk. The cold power windows sliding down at his touch, the faint thrum of a Harman Kardon stereo weaving sound around him like a velvet cloak.

But here? Here was the bus. The rattling, groaning cage. The smell of piss and vomit and human decay trapped like an invisible fog. The sticky strap digging into his palm. The faces, raw and rough and tired, all caught in this shared, relentless journey.

This was his new chariot.

The city rolling past the smeared windows was a blur of cracked sidewalks, peeling paint, graffiti crawling like vines over forgotten walls. Shadows stretched long and tired, as if even the sun wanted to give up.

Michael's mind wandered, spiraled.

The bus rattled and wheezed through the city streets, each bump and jolt pounding against Michael's ribs like a relentless reminder of his unraveling life. Outside the smeared windows, the world blurred into cracked pavement, flickering streetlights, and the graffiti-scarred faces of forgotten neighborhoods.

He tightened his grip on the sticky strap, eyes flicking to the small pull cord hanging limp beside the window. Nearing the car dealership—his intended destination—Michael's fingers trembled as he yanked the cord with a sharp tug.

Nothing.

No clatter. No ding. No flashing sign. The bus rumbled on, indifferent.

His jaw clenched. He pulled the cord again. The other passengers barely registered, lost in their own shadows. The driver's eyes remained fixed on the road, expression unreadable behind a scratched windshield.

The city's noise faded into a low, oppressive hum, broken only by the bus's labored breathing and the dull thud of his heart.

Michael pushed his way through the cramped aisle, apologizing silently, eyes downcast as his boots shuffled past indifferent bodies.

"Next stop, please," he muttered, voice low.

The bus passed the lot he'd planned to stop at, the one where hope met reality and rust chased dreams. The faded sign glowed faintly in the dusk, mocking.

He reached the door just as the bus creaked past the next stop.

The doors hissed open.

He stepped out into the warm afternoon sun, the heat pressing down like a weight. Sweat slicked his forehead and soaked the collar of his shirt as he turned away from the bus stop. The city smelled of dust and exhaust.

The gravel beneath his shoes crunched sharply with each step as he walked back several blocks, the sticky strap still clutched loosely in his hand. His breath came uneven, ragged in the thick air.

Chapter 10: Used Cars

Finally, the used car dealership came into view. It looked halfway decent—clean, organized, rows of sedans and SUVs lined up like soldiers on a sunbaked battlefield. Not a dented fender in sight. The smell of wax and gasoline mixed with the dry heat, swirling dust motes catching the light.

Michael's eyes flicked from one vehicle to another.

A silver Toyota Corolla, clean, no rust. The price tag: **$4,200**. Way out of range.

A well-kept Honda CR-V, its tires almost new, the paint shining despite the fading light. Price tag: **$5,000**.

His chest tightened. He moved on.

A beaten-up Ford Focus with a promising "Certified Pre-Owned" sticker, but the number in red on the windshield made his stomach drop. **$3,800**.

He bit his lip.

A door opened behind him, and a man stepped out.

Mid-forties, pressed khakis, neat haircut, and a smile polished enough to catch the dying light.

"Afternoon, sir," he said, extending a hand. "Welcome to Evans Used Cars. Looking for something reliable today?"

Michael shook his hand, trying to steady his voice. "Yeah. Reliable is good."

"Smart choice," the salesman said, walking alongside him. "Used car buying can be tricky, but we pride ourselves on quality here. No surprises."

Michael nodded. "That's good."

The salesman's tone grew warmer, more conversational. "You working around here?"

"Yeah. Got laid off recently," Michael admitted, feeling the words stick in his throat.

"Ah, that's rough. I hear ya. These days, gotta stretch every dollar. You got a budget in mind?"

Michael hesitated but decided to be honest. "Around twelve hundred, maybe a bit less."

The man stopped walking. His smile froze. For a long beat, the friendly salesman turned cold, his eyes narrowing slightly.

He let out a short, harsh laugh that didn't reach his eyes.

"$1,200?" he scoffed, shaking his head like Michael was a joke.

"Sir, we don't have anything close to that. That's not even pocket change around here." His voice dropped, thick with contempt.

Before Michael could respond, the salesman turned abruptly and strode back toward the air-conditioned office, leaving the door swinging open behind him.

Michael stood alone on the gravel, heat pressing down like a weight.

The cars gleamed around him, beautiful, expensive, and utterly out of reach.

The door to the office shut with a quiet finality.

He felt the sting of abandonment, sharp and bitter.

Chapter 11: Uncle Roy's Got Your Back

Michael stood in the gravel a few seconds longer, the sun pressing down like punishment. The door to the office was already closed — the conversation over, the verdict clear.

His steps back to the bus stop were heavy and deliberate. Heat shimmered off the cracked pavement, warping the world in waves that felt both unreal and inevitable. It wasn't just hot, it was accusatory, like the day itself had turned on him.

He boarded the bus without a word. The stale air slapped him, old rubber, sweat, and something metallic in the vents.

He grabbed a pole, sticky from too many hands and sank into a seat that coughed dust when he sat.

The bus rattled forward, and the city peeled by in layers, graffiti-tagged fences, sagging porches, windows sealed with cardboard. The city welcomed him, slow, silent, without judgement.

As they crossed into a rougher stretch of town, Michael saw it.

A crooked sign, half-lit by flickering neon, clung to the side of a sun-bleached shack of a building:

Uncle Roy's Used Car Emporium.

The lot sprawled before it like a graveyard no one bothered to bury, scattered with battered cars of every make and model.

Rusted grilles grinned like broken teeth, and sun-bleached paint curled away from metal like old skin.

A few hoods were popped open, frozen mid-defeat.

The bus hissed to a stop.

Michael stepped into the heat, his shoes crunching against gravel, dust rising and hanging in the air like cigarette smoke no one bothered to wave away.

He crossed the lot slowly.

Every car looked like it had a story, and none of them ended well.

A shattered rearview.

A windshield held together with packing tape.

A bumper zip-tied in place like a desperate stitch.

The building ahead leaned under its own weight. Its windows were fogged with grease, and the siding peeled like it had once tried to shed its own skin.

Painted slogans screamed from every direction:

"Best Deals in Town!"

"No Credit? No Problem!"

"Drive It Today, Pay It Tomorrow!"

A pulsating, inflatable clown wobbled erratically near the lot's entrance, its gaudy red nose and wide, toothy grin twisting in the stifling breeze like a carnival nightmare come to life. The plastic arms flailed wildly, grabbing for attention but offering no comfort.

Above it all, strings of cheap, multicolored pennants fluttered limply, their colors faded to pastel ghosts by the relentless sun.

Michael blinked against the harsh glare, the absurdity of it all sinking in. This was a different world from the gleaming, sanitized lots he'd known. This was raw and ragged, a circus of desperation and second chances.

The smell of gasoline mixed with burnt rubber and something off, like sweat and old regrets fermenting in the hot air.

He hesitated, swallowing the lump rising in his throat. This was the place he'd come to now. Another plateau of his slow, grinding descent.

Michael scanned the rows of cars again, hope flickering weakly with each glance. But the prices kept towering over his budget like taunting skyscrapers, $2,500 here, $3,200 there. Even the rusted relics wore price tags that felt like punches to the gut.

His shoulders slumped, the weight of it all pressing harder. This wasn't just a car lot; it was a battlefield where he was already losing.

Then, from the shadowed corner of the lot, a figure emerged.

Uncle Roy.

He shuffled forward with the unmistakable swagger of a man who had spent decades perfecting the art of selling broken dreams wrapped in glossy promises.

His greasy comb-over clung to a scalp that seemed to be surrendering ground faster than he could comb it. The part was impossibly low, like a crooked horizon on a bald plain.

A toothpick dangled lazily from the corner of his mouth, bobbing slightly as he talked to himself under his breath.

Roy's suit... or was it an outdated leisure suit? The fabric clung tight in some places, loose and baggy in others, as if decades of bad tailoring and bad decisions had come together in a single garment.

The pale pastel shirt beneath was stained in places Michael didn't want to identify.

His scuffed loafers clicked against the gravel, announcing his approach like a bad joke about to be told.

Roy's eyes gleamed with a greasy charm as he locked onto Michael, flashing a grin that promised everything and nothing all at once.

"Howdy, amigo," he drawled.

"Looking for a real deal, or just killing time?"

Michael said nothing, still staring down at a dented sedan with peeling paint.

Roy took a step closer, wiping his hands on his ill-fitting leisure suit. "I can tell you're a discerning gentleman with impeccable taste," he said, voice dripping with false sincerity. "Not just some guy looking for any old bucket. You want quality, you want style, you want *value*."

He winked exaggeratedly, toothpick bobbing. "And that's exactly what I'm here to give you."

Michael's eyes flicked back up, meeting Roy's slick gaze. He wanted to believe the pitch, but the sinking feeling in his gut told him this was just another act —

the kind of show that left you clinging to hope while your wallet got picked clean.

Roy continued, "Don't let those shiny lots fool you, friend. They play the game by *their* rules — prices out the roof, slick suits, fancy coffee. Here? We play it straight. Real deals for real people."

He stretched out a hand, palm up, as if sealing a secret pact.

Michael hesitated, weighing the honesty against the smell of grease and desperation in the air.

Michael glanced at Roy's outstretched hand but didn't take it. Instead, he folded his arms, his eyes narrowing slightly.

"Real deals for real people, huh?" Michael said, voice low. "Sounds good. But I've seen plenty of deals. Mostly, they end up with me paying for a car that won't start."

Roy chuckled, a sound that was part amusement, part practiced charm. "Ah, that's where you're wrong, my friend. You're not buying a car; you're buying peace of mind. You want a ride that gets you from point A to point B without a hiccup. And Uncle Roy's got just that."

He gestured broadly to the lot, the collection of beaten-up dreams. "Sure, some of these beauties have a story, but hey, who doesn't? It's not about perfection. It's about *promise*."

Michael looked down again at the cars peeling paint and cracked windshields.

Roy leaned in, lowering his voice like he was sharing the secret of the century. "And between you and me, amigo, I might have something just right for your budget."

Michael's eyes lifted, a flicker of hope kindling despite himself.

Roy smiled wide, "Let's take a walk."

Roy threw his hands up like a showman unveiling the crown jewel. "Now, this baby? She's a real cream puff. Owned by a sweet little old lady from Peoria, Illinois. Best friends with my late wife, God rest her soul. Used to drive it to bingo twice a week. Nothing rough, just gentle rides to keep her mind sharp."

He gave the Pinto a fond pat, ignoring the peeling panel and the rust creeping at the wheel wells.

"Only 75,000 miles on the clock," Roy added with a wink, "and that wear and tear? Pure character. You don't see cars like this anymore."

Michael's eyes flicked back to the cracked tires, sunk deep into the gravel like they'd been parked there for months, dust layered thick enough to write a story in.

Roy, sensing hesitation, pushed on. "Just got it yesterday, too. Fresh on the lot. You're the first to see her, amigo."

Michael bit his tongue, swallowing the urge to call out the obvious lies. The evidence was all there, the dust, the settled tires, the smell that clung to the cracked window. But he wasn't in a position to argue.

He nodded slowly, trying to convince himself that maybe, just maybe, Roy's words held a sliver of truth.

Roy leaned in, voice dropping to a conspiratorial whisper, the toothpick bobbing as he spoke.

"Now this baby's a classic. Worth hundreds more, no doubt. But you know what? I like you. I can see you're a good man."

He paused, eyes locking onto Michael's with a sly grin.

"I'm going to break a promise I made to myself and let you have her for just fifteen hundred bucks. Cash, of course."

He clapped his hands together, like sealing a secret deal between two allies in a crooked game.

"You won't find a better price anywhere. This is a steal, amigo."

Michael's jaw tightened. Fifteen hundred dollars. Cash. That was everything he had set aside for a car, and then some. He glanced back at the Pinto, its cracked windows and peeling paint mocking him silently.

"Fifteen hundred," he repeated, voice low.

Roy nodded eagerly, sensing the hesitation. "I'm telling you, this is your chance. No credit checks, no waiting, no hassle. Just sign here, here, and here."

He pulled out a clipboard with a stack of papers, the forms crisp and official-looking but heavy with fine print.

Michael's eyes flicked over the documents, each line blurring together under the weight of the decision.

Part of him screamed to walk away, to hold on to what little dignity remained. But the other part, the part battered and broken by months of losing everything, whispered, *What choice do you have?*

Roy leaned in, voice oily and persuasive. "You're making the smart move, amigo. Trust me. This baby's got a few miles left in her, and so do you."

Michael swallowed hard, took a deep breath, and reached for the pen.

Michael eased the Pinto into gear, the engine coughing awake like an old man clearing his throat. Dust swirled behind the car as he rolled off the gravel lot, the sun beating down mercilessly.

In the rearview mirror, Roy stood waving — his toothpick bobbing with every nod, that slick, greasy grin stretched wide across his face.

Michael watched him shrink in the glass, but the smile lingered, smeared across the heat like something that wouldn't wash off.

Roy had the fifteen hundred in hand, and his eyes were twitching with anticipation, not for bills or repairs, but for whatever vices came quickest.

A longshot at the track.

A warm body behind a locked door in a cheap motel room paid by the hour.

Whiskey in a paper bag.

A man burning through luck the way others burn through gas, fast, reckless, and always needing more.

Michael exhaled and tightened his grip on the cracked steering wheel. The heat in the Pinto was rising, the vinyl seats sticking to his back. Ahead, the road shimmered like something alive and waiting.

He didn't look back again. He knew what was behind him.

Chapter 12: Four Score and a Box of Shame

He stepped through the automatic doors of the discount grocery store, cradling the ragged and stained cardboard box against his chest like a fragile relic. It wasn't heavy, but it had that awkward shape that made it impossible to carry with dignity.

Inside: a box of macaroni and cheese, not the artisanal kind made with Gruyère or Comté. No, this was the kind born from the unholy matrimony of limp, overboiled noodles and a foil packet of neon orange industrial powder. A chemical event masquerading as cheese. It smelled faintly of regret and reeked of cost-cutting, the culinary equivalent of a clown crying in a parking lot.

Beneath that: generic saltine crackers and a can of something called *"potted meat"* — which he'd only grabbed because it was cheap and the label leaned with great optimism toward the word *MEAT*, bold and centered like a promise it had no intention of keeping. He didn't even know what it was, exactly. Some kind of gray-brown paste, he figured — a slurry of bygone animals, finely pureed until no trace of species, texture, or dignity remained. Probably laced with marrow dust, snouts, glands, and whatever sinewy leftovers could be coaxed from a power hose into a slaughterhouse drain.

It was meat in theory. The label was confident, even if the contents weren't.

And yet it sat in his box, his pantry of defeat, heavy with preservatives, lies, and just enough salt to outlast a nuclear event.

The blast of air conditioning disappeared the moment the sliding doors whooshed shut behind him. The heat hit him like a wall, flat and grimy, the kind of summer heat that didn't burn so much as it pressed, like a hand on your neck.

He paused just outside, adjusting his grip on the box, eyeing the distant shimmer of his Pinto wagon parked crooked at the far end of the lot. The paint was sun-bleached and dull, the fake wood grain peeling in long, curling strips. One of the hubcaps was missing, and the other three were fighting to stay.

The "store" behind him didn't look like a place where you shopped. It looked like a place where you admitted defeat. A final stop on the long, slow descent from aspiration to survival.

A mausoleum of dignity. A cathedral of lowered expectations. A palace of broken dreams dressed up in fluorescent lighting and dust. Aisles shuffled through by the living dead.

He trudged across the parking lot like a man returning from war, only instead of medals and glory, he carried sodium-packed shame and a can of questionable meat. Each step toward the Pinto wagon echoed hollowly in his head.

It wasn't that long ago he'd been sliding into Italian leather seats, brushing the dust off a mahogany console in his Range Rover. Back when grocery bags were packed for him in biodegradable hemp totes from Whole Foods. Back when dinner was prime rib, not this cardboard box of edible regret.

He shifted the box in his arms as it began to buckle under its own dampness. One of the flaps gave way slightly, revealing the corner of a crushed off-brand cereal box and a dented can of creamed corn. He swallowed the lump in his throat. It tasted like rust and shame.

The Pinto came into full view: rust creeping up from the wheel wells, faux wood grain flayed from the passenger side like sunburned skin. A tangled cassette adapter dangled from the radio, like some primitive medical device trying to shock a dead decade back to life.

This was where he'd landed. From curated Spotify playlists to AM talk radio and cassette tapes labeled "Road Jams '97." From imported scotch to potted meat.

He sighed again. Deeper this time.

And that's when he heard it—tires crunching slowly across gravel. A low engine hum. Laughter. A car pulling in behind him.

He turned.

And there they were.

The Lincoln Navigator rolled up slowly behind him—gleaming, monstrous, absurd in its self-importance. Chrome everywhere. Tinted windows that reflected the miserable heatwaves off the blacktop like some kind of luxury mirage.

It idled there for a second, engine humming smooth and arrogant.

Then the driver's side window began to glide down with an effortless electric sigh.

And there they were.

Her sunglasses were oversized, her lips glossed, her expression too casual to be accidental. She was leaning over slightly from the passenger seat, one elbow propped on the window's edge like she hadn't planned it—like the whole thing was just chance.

Next to her, grinning behind the wheel, was Bobby Lincoln.

His arm hung lazily over the steering wheel, his hair shorter than he remembered, styled like he cared a lot about things like hair. A smug little smirk played across his face like the punchline to a joke only he could hear.

"Hey!" she called out, feigning surprise with just enough delay to make it sting. "Wow. You look… different."

The box in his arms sagged as the bottom began to give, a can of creamed corn shifting dangerously near the edge. He adjusted it with a jerk, trying to hold it, and himself together.

He gave a shallow nod, jaw tight, eyes flicking from her glossed smile to Bobby Lincoln's shit-eating grin behind the wheel.

It hadn't been forever. It had barely been a month.

But standing there, in the hot breath of the parking lot with a box of off-brand misery and a Pinto wagon waiting behind him, it may as well have been a lifetime.

She leaned just a little closer to the open window, her voice light but dripping with that clipped sweetness he knew all too well.

"So… how've you been? Still driving that thing?" Her eyes flicked to the Pinto like it was a punchline, and she smirked.

He tightened his grip on the box, knuckles white. "Yeah," he said, voice rough, "still gets me where I need to go."

Lincoln laughed, low and easy, like a cat that's just knocked over the expensive vase and knows he's untouchable.

"Hey, don't be so hard on the classics," Bobby said, flashing a grin full of polished teeth and privilege. "That wagon's got character."

Character. The word hit him like a slap. He glanced down at the peeling fake wood grain and the rust creeping up the side, like a sickness he couldn't shake.

His ex's gaze softened for a moment, almost pitying, but just for a second. Then she caught Lincoln's eye and leaned back, laughter bubbling up between them.

"Still eating those gourmet meals, huh?" she teased, nodding toward the box. "What's that stuff anyway? Potted meat?"

He blinked, heat rushing to his face. "It's… food."

Something in him snapped.

"You know what? Fuck off."

He didn't wait for a response. Turning, he started loading his treasures into the car, the cardboard box creaking under the weight of his defeat.

Behind him, the power windows slid up with smooth, taunting finality. The Navigator rolled away, a growl of polished power cutting through the summer heat.

He caught the faint chorus of laughter chasing after him, sharp, cruel, alive.

His knuckles whitened as he shifted the box into the cracked passenger seat. He slammed the door shut and sank into the driver's seat, the worn vinyl groaning beneath him.

On instinct, he reached for the window crank, trying to roll it down, and the handle snapped clean off in his hand.

He stared at it, dumbfounded for half a second, then hurled it to the passenger side floor. "Fucking piece of shit."

He gritted his teeth, fists clenched tight on the steering wheel. "Bigshot asshole," he muttered, voice low and ragged. "Fucking spoiled prick in his shiny-ass Lincoln, acting like the king of the world. Got his whole damn life handed to him on a silver platter."

His eyes flicked to the peeling fake wood grain on the door panel. "And her—God, what the hell was she thinking? Trading me in for that ugly fuck. Big man, big ego, no class."

The Pinto wheezed as he pulled out of the lot, the radio crackling with some sad bastard's country song about lost love and empty bottles. He snorted bitterly. "Yeah, well, enjoy your navigator, assholes."

As he rolled down the cracked pavement, his voice dropped to a low mumble, a litany of curses and spite aimed at everything that had slipped through his fingers. Winding his way home, he braced for a feast fit for a trainyard vagrant…a sorry spread of potted meat on dry crackers and a quart of Rhinelander—the kind of meal that poisoned the soul more than it nourishes the body.

His fist slammed the steering wheel, rattling the brittle dashboard. "Fuck 'em all."

Chapter 13: Dining on Crow

Michael shuffled through the front door with the cardboard box balanced in his arms like an offering no one wanted. The bottom was beginning to give. A damp patch had spread out into a sagging belly of soft paperboard. The smell followed, a waft that landed somewhere between sour milk and something worse.

He kicked the door shut behind him and set the box down on the kitchen table.

Inside: the spoils of surrender.

He unpacked them one by one, laying them out like sacred artifacts from a failed excavation.

First came the box of macaroni and cheese. The brand name was a vague imitation spelled like a lawsuit waiting to happen. Then the potted meat. It shimmered under the kitchen light like a cursed relic, the label blaspheming the word *MEAT* with grotesque certainty — mocking him from the shadows of his own kitchen.

A bottle of fruit punch that claimed to contain "citrus essence" and boasted proudly *No Real Juice!*

A half-loaf of white bread, smashed flat, edges yellowed. A jar of pickled eggs floating in what looked like formaldehyde.

Next came the creamed corn, dented can, generic label. He twisted the opener. It let out a faint *pfft* of air and despair. The contents slithered out in a slow-motion plop, a sludge more cream than corn. Beige with faint yellow chunks clinging to life.

He stared at the mess. No, not mess — dinner.

It was a still life of the bottom rung. A banquet of sodium and sadness. He told himself that it was bad, but it was temporary. He'd bounce back.

He reached for the can of meat spread. No opener required, the label bragged about that too. "Easy Peel Lid!" Like they were doing him a favor. He peeled it back. It made a *suck-pop* noise as it released.

The smell hit him like a bad memory.

And finally, the wine.

Not in a bottle but a convenient box. The brand was something along the lines of *Desperate Vineyards* printed in faded, romantic script. He pressed the plastic spout, and it belched out a dark syrupy stream, thick, warm, and slightly foamy. It hit the bottom of the glass with a sickly splatter.

He swirled it once, ironically, then took a sip. He remembered tasting notes in days gone by. Terms like dark red fruit, vanilla, chocolate, hints of lavender, silky tannins.

Today, none of those seemed to apply. This was sharper, more direct. Grape jelly, expired cough syrup, alcohol, and a hint of something decomposing.

Still, it was different. And that counted for something.

He'd been living on gas station cheeseburgers. Mixed meat pucks with rehydrated onions sweating in flameproof paper under heat lamps. Not gourmet but functional, affordable.

At least this was a meal. Albeit a tragic one. A parody of yesterday. But it was food with steps.

He boiled the macaroni. Dumped in the powder. Stirred. The noodles clumped together like they'd made a pact against him. The "cheese" didn't melt so much as coat. The lumpy powder surrendered into an orange liquid that clung to the spoon like a warning.

He spooned it into a cracked bowl and added a dollop of potted meat on top like a garnish from hell.

The first bite was hot, salty, and utterly flavorless.

The second had a gamey tang, probably the meat.

The third he didn't taste at all.

He chewed out of obligation, not hunger. A man performing the ritual of sustenance.

When the bowl was halfway gone, he stood up and poured himself more wine. It sputtered from the box like an old wound reopening.

He sat back at the table to reengage the meal as if it were a combatant. The textures clashed in his mouth as he chewed, soggy noodles oozing orange liquid, clumps of unforgiving flesh paste refusing to yield.

He sipped after each bite. His mind wandered.

He remembered those candlelit meals with Kayla, Wagyu filets, imported wine, her senseless ramblings disguised as conversation, and his ridiculous responses disguised as interest.

It had all been a performance. A fucking audition for a life neither of them even wanted.

This meal was the epitome of defeat, cold, callous, but honest.

The bitter taste softened as he swallowed.

Chapter 14: Revelations

Part One: The Break In

The headlights of the car sliced through the falling twilight, casting long shadows that danced across the cracked pavement. The engine hummed low, a background noise to the thumping in his chest. His eyes were glazed, fixed on the houses around him, rows of quiet, unsuspecting homes, all wrapped in the same suburban monotony. It was the same every night. He wasn't sure what he was looking for, but he knew when he'd found it.

A flicker of light in the corner of his eye. A house, similar to the others with a sprinkler system running on the front lawn. The front porch light was on but the house looked dark inside.

He turned the wheel sharply, pulling off the main road and into a parking lot hidden in the shadows. The car came to a stop with a soft squeak of the brakes. For a moment, he left the engine running, the faint glow of the dashboard illuminating his fingers, twitching slightly as he gripped the wheel. He didn't need to think much. This wasn't the time for hesitation. He threw the door open, the heat of the day was giving in to the cooling night air as he stepped onto the asphalt.

He didn't hurry, he never did. There was no rush, no need for it. His feet crunched lightly against the gravel as he headed toward the alley that ran behind the house. The alley was narrow, dark, and smelled faintly of old trash and wet concrete. His shoes made little sound against the uneven ground, the occasional clink of loose stones the only noise that seemed to break the silence. He moved with the ease of someone who had walked this path before, there was a rhythm to it, almost mechanical, the way his body shifted in the shadows, barely noticeable.

His eyes flicked around, taking in the details, an old broom leaning against the fence, a couple of boxes piled up in the corner, a loose sheet of plastic fluttering in the wind. He felt a strange sense of calm in this space, like an extension of his own being. The world around felt muffled, softened by the shelter of the alley, the trees overhead blocking out the stars.

He reached the house without breaking his stride. He was in luck, no one outside. He slipped through the gate confidently. Anyone watching would believe he belonged. As he approached the back of the house he slid behind a cluster of overgrown bushes. His fingers brushed against the rough bark as he crouched low. The dark colors of his clothing were swallowed by the surrounding flora. He could see inside, just enough. The dim light entering from the window pooled onto the tile floor. He could tell the place was empty, no movement, no sounds.

He stayed close against the wall as he eased along the back of the house. The door was just a few feet away now. He crouched, pulled a flathead screwdriver from his coat, and slid it into the seam near the handle.

A pause. A breath. The sound of rustling leaves.

He leaned in, applying pressure, not brute force, just the right kind of persuasion. The screwdriver flexed, bit, twisted.

A dull pop echoed like a bone giving way.

The door sagged inward an inch, hinges whining softly in protest. He caught it before it could swing too far, guiding it open with slow, practiced hands.

Not quiet. Not clean. But effective.

And just like that, he was inside.

The air inside smelled fresh, clean, not something he was used to. He paused for a moment, listening, letting his senses adjust to the space. The kitchen was just ahead. His eyes skimmed the countertops, empty, save for a few scattered papers and a chipped mug. The fridge sat there, unassuming, as though it had been waiting for him.

Without hesitation, he opened it. The escaping cold air hit him. Inside, it was almost comically bare. A jar of mustard, its label faded and peeling. A quart of milk. And there, tucked in the back—an unmarked plastic container. He frowned, lifting it carefully from the shelf.

It looked like meat. Kind of. The color was off, gray, like something that had been left out too long. He opened it slowly, the smell that hit him brought back memories of feeding his childhood dog. But hunger gnawed at him. He used his finger, scooping a bit of the strange substance, bringing it to his mouth without thinking.

The texture was wrong. Slimy, almost. It sat on his tongue for a moment before he even registered the taste. His stomach lurched.

He froze.

Then he saw it, sitting innocently on the counter. A can. Potted meat. He blinked, disgust creeping in, as he spat the gray mess out into the sink. *What the fuck is this?*

He wiped his mouth with the back of his hand, shaking his head in disbelief. *This guy eats worse than me— and I'm a fucking junkie.*

He wiped his hand on his jeans, sneering at the aftertaste still clinging to the back of his throat. The fridge door swung shut behind him with a dull thud. He took one last look at the sad kitchen—cheap linoleum floors, old white cabinets, a calendar on the wall with some long-forgotten success slogan. Too wholesome. Too clean. It made his skin crawl a little.

Then the hunt began.

He moved fast, practiced, but left wreckage in his wake. The drawers under the counter were yanked out and dumped upside down onto the floor—forks, receipts, broken pens scattered across the linoleum. A basket of neatly arranged mail was flipped and kicked aside. Anything that didn't look immediately valuable was tossed, broken, or simply left in a pile of debris.

Into the living room next, he swept an entire row of books off the coffee table with one arm, barely glancing at the covers before stepping over them. The couch cushions were torn from their frames and thrown across the room. A small side lamp crashed to the floor with a sharp pop, bulb shattering like brittle ice.

His eyes darted everywhere, fingers always moving, open, search, discard, repeat. He didn't slow down. That was part of the process. Quick hands. No lingering.

By the time he reached the hallway, the kitchen looked like it had been hit by a storm.

The office wasn't spared. He ripped open the desk drawers, dumping their contents onto the rug, paper clips, notebooks, a USB stick, some yellowing receipts. Nothing of real value.

In the bedroom, the destruction became almost surgical. He moved like a machine, nightstand drawers yanked and overturned, the mattress flipped halfway off the bed, sheets twisted and dragging on the floor. The closet was gutted. Hangers flew. Neatly folded clothes ended up in crumpled piles. A pair of shoes went skittering across the hardwood as he searched for hidden compartments behind the shelves, inside the baseboards, behind the vents.

He didn't just *search*, he *disassembled*.

In the bathroom, he tore through the medicine cabinet, knocking a toothbrush holder into the sink where it shattered into three jagged pieces. Towels yanked from racks. Toilet tank lid lifted, checked, dropped with a hollow bang.

Still nothing.

He paused only once, standing amid the chaos, breathing harder now. Every room behind him looked

85

like it had been raided by a lunatic, but he wasn't careless. He was efficient. Fast. He just didn't care what the place looked like after. Why would he?

All he cared about was the score.

He was back in the kitchen, stepping over the mess he'd made, drawers flung out like broken jaws, silverware scattered like bones. His mind was already back in the game, trying to figure where this square bastard might've hidden the real valuables, when his phone buzzed in his pocket.

The sound made him flinch.

He yanked it out, thumbed the screen. Blocked number. He already knew who it was.

"Yeah?" he answered, voice low, eyes still scanning the room.

A familiar voice, cold and razor-sharp, crackled through the line.

"Do you have my money?"

He ran a hand through his greasy hair. "I'm working on it as we speak," he muttered, stepping toward the counter. His eyes were darting around now, suddenly more focused, more alert. The calm he had before was gone, replaced by that creeping itch that always came when money was on the line.

"We're not playing here," the voice said. **"I need you to meet me tomorrow night. Ten o'clock. Parking lot at 189 East Lincoln. If you don't show, consider yourself done. I'm serious, man. Real serious."**

His heart was pounding now, not from fear—but from that kind of wired adrenaline that only comes when everything's closing in. "Okay, okay—Lincoln, Lincoln..." He spun in place, looking for something to write with. "Hang on, what's the number again?"

There, on the counter. A large white notepad, clean, probably used for grocery lists or polite reminders. He grabbed it.

Nothing to write with.

He glanced down, on the floor, half under the fridge door, a fat black marker. Probably for labeling freezer bags or writing big block letters on moving boxes. He snatched it up and uncapped it with his teeth.

"Lincoln, what's the number?" he said again, flipping the pad open and scrawling the street name in large, uneven letters:

LINCOLN

He was writing big, like he needed to *see* it to remember.

And that's when he heard it.

The sound of tires turning on pavement. A car pulling into the driveway. Headlights flared briefly against the curtains before vanishing into shadow. The sound of an engine idling just outside the house.

He froze, marker still in his hand, the scent of sharp black ink heavy in the air. The phone still against his ear.

"Shit," he hissed into the phone. "Sorry, man—I gotta run. Call you back."

He hung up without waiting for a reply, jamming the phone deep into his pocket. His heartbeat was in his throat now, loud as a drum. No time to collect notes. He would follow up with the dealer later. Now he had to make his escape.

He moved quick but quiet through the house, stepping over overturned cushions and scattered books. The place looked like it had been turned inside out, no time to fix it. No point. He eased the back door open just enough to slip through, careful not to let it creak.

The panic was there but he contained it. By the time he hit the backyard, he looked like just any other homeowner. Shoulders loose. Expression blank. Hands in his pockets. Nothing to see here.

But his legs were moving fast. Not running. Not quite. But close.

As he cleared the back gate, he slipped into the shadows of the alley like a ghost.

As soon as he was out of view, he broke into a full sprint—shoes slapping the pavement, breath sharp in his throat, eyes fixed ahead. The alley blurred around him, fences, trash cans, the dark backs of garages. He didn't stop. Not until he saw his car.

There. Waiting where he left it.

He yanked the door open, threw himself inside, and twisted the key in one motion. The engine growled awake.

No headlights.

Just reverse.

He backed out slow at first, then gunned it the second his wheels hit the street. Tires hissed. The car surged forward and disappeared into the night, taillights vanishing like dying embers.

Part Two: The Message

The door creaked as he pushed it open.

At first, it didn't register. just a sense that something was... off. The air felt wrong. Still. Not quiet, but suspended, like the house was holding its breath.

He stepped inside.

The lights were off, but faint twilight filtered in through the blinds. A couch cushion lay face-down on the floor. One of the dining chairs was toppled sideways. A drawer yawned open in the hallway like a broken jaw.

His breath caught in his chest.

"What the hell..." he whispered, barely audible.

He stepped forward, slowly, his shoes crunching on something, paper? Glass?

The living room was torn apart. Books scattered. Shelves emptied. The lamp was shattered, bulb fragments glittering like poison stars on the floor. The couch cushions were gutted and tossed.

His pace quickened.

Kitchen next. Drawers open. Cabinets ajar. Food pulled from shelves and scattered onto the counter and floor below. His old mug from work lay in pieces beneath the counter. His name still half-visible on one of the shards.

He turned in a slow circle, eyes wide, mind stuttering.

But nothing was taken.

Not the TV. Not his phone charging on the kitchen table. Not the cheap jewelry in the bedroom. The place had been gutted, but not robbed. Just... violated.

"Why... why would someone..."

And then he saw it.

On the counter. In the center of the chaos. A clean white notepad.

One word.

Written in thick, blocky strokes, like it had been carved into the page with hate.

LINCOLN

Michael stared at the notepad.

Just one word. One thick, black, intrusive word.

LINCOLN.

The letters were jagged, uneven, scrawled with urgency, like a threat or a confession or a curse. It was so absurd, so out of place, he almost laughed. But his throat didn't work. His mouth was dry. His eyes didn't blink.

Why?

It hung there like smoke. In the kitchen. In his skull.

His fingers hovered over the paper, not touching it, just... hovering. As if contact might set something off. As if it was radioactive.

"What the fuck is that supposed to mean?"

His voice sounded wrong. Too loud. Thin. Echoing off the tile like a scream in a tomb.

He took a step back.

Then another.

Turned slowly in a circle, scanning the wreckage of his home—bookshelves overturned, drawers gutted, couch cushions disemboweled like livestock in a ritual slaughter.

But nothing was missing. Nothing taken.

This wasn't a robbery.

His breath caught. A cold bloom opened in his chest.

This was a message.

He staggered back against the fridge, the corner of it slamming into his spine, but he didn't feel it. He was staring past the broken lamp, past the torn-up floor mats, past the chaos to that one fucking word on the counter.

LINCOLN.

And then—

Then the flood came.

His mind began to race.

Not just fast, **unhinged**. Like every synapse fired at once and none of them in order.

Lincoln.

Lincoln.

Lincoln Talon Acquisitions. That was the name on the fucking layoff letter.

Lincoln Automotive. That was stamped on the tow truck paperwork.

And now Kayla. **Bobby Lincoln.** That smirking, pasty-faced dickhead from high school with a trust fund and a chin like a melted ice cube.

It wasn't just coincidence. No way. Not now. Not this.

"No. No fucking way. What is this?"

He spun in place, palms to his temples, pacing tight circles in the wrecked kitchen like a man on a prison yard.

"What is this?!" he shouted again, voice cracking.

He stormed into the living room—books still scattered, the coffee table skewed. His eyes flicked to the wall, to the mirror Kayla had picked out from some boutique he couldn't afford even when he had a job.

He saw his reflection and didn't recognize it.

Red face. Wild eyes. Something broken blooming behind his pupils.

Then the rage came.

Sudden. Sharp. White-hot.

He grabbed the **heavy ceramic potted plant** by the window, Kayla's stupid idea, some overpriced monstera that never grew right, and with a grunt, **hurled it at the wall**.

Crash.

A burst of ceramic. A wet smear of dirt. A crater in the drywall.

He stood there, chest heaving.

He didn't stop.

"You think this is funny?" he barked into the empty house. "You think this is some kind of fucking game?"

He stormed into the kitchen, eyes landing on the **wooden chair** tucked neatly under the table, till intact, still civilized, like the world hadn't just declared war on him.

He grabbed it with both hands.

SLAM.

Right onto the table. The legs bounced.

SLAM.

Harder this time. The wood cracked.

SLAM.

The chair exploded on the third hit—legs splintering, one of them flying across the room and knocking a framed photo off the counter. The glass shattered, spraying across the linoleum in a constellation of glinting pieces.

He stood over the wreckage, panting. A thread of spit dangled from his lip like a rabid dog. He wiped it away with the back of his hand.

Then the questions started, **loud, accusatory, desperate**:

"What do you want from me?"
"Who are you?!"
"What did I do, huh? What the fuck did I do!?"

He staggered backward, knocking into the fridge. His hand found the countertop, gripping it for balance.

The kitchen was spinning. The house moaned under its own silence.

He stared down at the floor, shards of chair, broken pottery, smeared dirt, cracked glass.

It looked like a **crime scene**. But the crime wasn't over. It was **happening**.

He stayed there, **on his knees**, the carpet rough against his skin, chest heaving like he'd just run a mile. Around him, the house lay gutted, drawers emptied, lamps shattered, furniture knocked crooked like a scene out of a war zone.

And in the middle of it all: **him**.

He didn't move. He just stared. Not at anything specific, just through it all. Through the walls, through the mess, through himself.

The rage had burned hot and fast, but now something colder seeped in. A creeping, slow ache.

His fingers unclenched. He let his hands rest, limp, palms up, like he was waiting for something to fall into them.
Nothing did.

The silence returned. That familiar, padded, **Dublin-suburb silence**. Except now it felt... wrong. Like the air itself had shifted, warped around him. Like the house no longer recognized him. Like **he** no longer belonged here.

Chapter 15: The Morning After

Light filtered through the mangled blinds, bent, hanging sideways, one slat missing completely. It cast uneven stripes across the living room like a broken barcode. Anyone from the street could see in now, but Michael didn't care. Not anymore.

He opened his eyes slowly.

No alarm. No urgency. Just a low, steady buzz in the back of his skull, like his brain was still rebooting from a power surge.

He lay still on the couch for a moment, eyes fixed on the ceiling. It had a barely perceivable water stain he hadn't noticed before. Or maybe it had always been there, and he just never looked long enough. Either way, he stared at them like they held the answer to something.

Then he sat up. No stretch. No sigh. Just movement.

His flip-flops slapped softly against the wreckage as he made his way toward the kitchen, stepping over broken glass, crumpled papers, and the bent remains of what used to be a lamp. The floor creaked but he didn't slow down.

He reached the counter and stood there, silent.

Where once a gleaming Italian espresso machine sat, chrome polished, steaming milk hissing like a dragon, now there was only an empty space. A faint rectangle of cleaner countertop where it used to live.

Sold, maybe. Or thrown out. He couldn't remember. Didn't matter.

He turned on the faucet. Cold tap water flowed, clear and steady. He let it run for a moment longer than needed, then filled a chipped mug without checking for dust.

From a cabinet missing its door, he pulled down a jar of instant coffee. Twisted the lid. No measuring— just a rough dump into the mug.

He looked around. No spoon.

He bent down and picked up a pen lying among a pile of receipts and torn mail. It was cracked down the side, maybe leaking a little, but it still moved. He used it to stir the thick coffee-sludge slowly, patiently.

Then he took a sip.

It tasted bitter and gritty. But he didn't wince.

He took another.

He moved to the toaster without urgency.

It sat crooked on the counter, one side dented like it had been dropped, or thrown. He didn't remember doing it, but then again, last night blurred like a fever dream.

He reached into a half-crushed bag of bread, white, cheap, the kind he used to walk past at Whole Foods with a sneer. Two slices. Slightly smushed but still intact.

He dropped them in.

No butter. No plate. Just the mechanical hum of the old toaster coming to life, one red coil at a time.

He leaned against the counter and took another sip of his coffee-ink mixture, eyes scanning the wreckage.

A chair on its side. A potted plant ruptured against the far wall; soil spilled across the floor like blood from a head wound. Splinters. Books torn from shelves. A ripped dress shirt hanging from the ceiling fan.

He looked at it all without emotion.

The toaster clicked. The toast rose.

He pulled it out barehanded, too numb to feel the heat, and carried both slices in one hand to what was left of the dining area.

He didn't fix anything.

He just lowered himself into the debris, onto what used to be a chair, now a frame with a half-attached cushion, and began eating the toast in small, even bites.

No rush. No reaction. Just chewing.

By noon the sunlight had shifted, spotlighting the wreckage like a crime scene.

Michael wandered the house barefoot, the soles of his flip-flops grinding against broken glass and splintered wood. If it hurt, he didn't notice. If he was bleeding, he didn't care.

He opened the fridge, stared into its sterile glow, and closed it again. He turned on the tap and let it run brown for a few seconds before shutting it off. Looked out the window. Pulled the blinds shut, though they barely moved, bent, twisted, like everything else.

He stood in the center of the room and turned in a slow circle, eyes passing over the wreckage, the upturned chair, the shattered lamp, the marker still on the counter.

At some point, he sat on the floor.

He pulled his phone from the couch cushions and stared at the screen. No new messages. Just dust smudges and a crack near the corner.

He scrolled, slowly, like he was reading a dead language. His thumb stopped on a name he hadn't touched in months.

Joseph.

He hesitated for just a second, then tapped *Call.*

It rang four times.

Then:

"**Joseph.**"

"Joseph."

There was a pause. A shift in the air.

"…Michael?"

Another pause. Then:

"Jesus, man. It's been a minute. Everything alright?"

Michael opened his mouth but nothing came out at first. He looked around the wreckage of the living room, the broken chair, the cold cup still on the table.

"I don't know," he said finally. His voice sounded dry, like it had traveled too far to reach him.

Joseph didn't speak for a second. Then:

"You okay? You sound—"

"I'm fine."

A beat.

"I'm not fine."

Michael let out a long breath. His head tilted back against the wall.

"There's… been a lot. I lost my job. Kayla left. My car's gone. I think someone broke into my house. I—" He cut himself off. His hand trembled slightly.

Joseph exhaled, a low rustle over the line.

"Christ, Mike. That's a hell of a list."
He paused, then added, more softly,
"You alright? I mean—are *you* alright?"

Michael let out a dry laugh. "I don't even know what that means anymore."

Another silence, heavier this time.

Joseph's voice came through again, steadier. "Start from the beginning. What happened?"

Michael swallowed. He rubbed a hand over his face, leaving a smear of dust across his cheek.

"It started with the job," he said. "Company got bought out. Lincoln Talon Acquisitions."

Joseph made a vague noise of recognition, like he'd heard of it in passing.

"They let a bunch of us go. Gave me a mug and a fucking mousepad like some… parting gift."

Michael stood up slowly and paced toward the window. The sun outside made the wreckage seem almost theatrical, too bright.

"I came home, tried to keep it together. Didn't tell Kayla right away. But it didn't matter. She was already halfway gone."

A pause.

"She left me for this guy. Bobby Lincoln."

Joseph's tone sharpened. "Lincoln again?"

Michael didn't answer at first. Then, low: "Yeah. It's all Lincoln. It's always Lincoln."

Joseph was quiet.

Michael kept talking, the dam cracked now.

"And then the car. Repossessed. Tow truck had *Lincoln Recovery* printed on the side. And then—then someone broke in. Tore this place apart. But they didn't take anything. They just left a note."

"What kind of note?"

Michael looked down at the counter. At the word still scrawled there in thick black ink.

"Just one word," he said. "*Lincoln.*"

"Who would break into a house, steal nothing, and leave a note like that?"

Joseph let out a breath through his nose. Careful now.

"Michael... I mean, it's a common name. Lincoln. Could just be bad luck. Shit timing."

"No... no, no, no, no," Michael said, shaking his head even though Joseph couldn't see it. "You don't get it. It's not just the job. Or the car. Or Kayla. It's... *all* of it. And they're all tied to Lincoln. I didn't see it at first either."

His voice cracked.

"You know what Dad used to say — there's no such thing as coincidences. What are the odds?"

There was a long pause.

Joseph said nothing.

Michael let out a shaky laugh.
"This is some kind of cosmic fuck-you."

Joseph's voice came back low and cautious.
"Mike… are you sleeping?"

"Not really."

"Are you—using anything?"

Michael barked a humorless laugh.
"Jesus. No."

"Okay," Joseph said. Still calm, but now every word came like it was being weighed before leaving his mouth.
"Because you're starting to sound… off, man. Like, really off."

Michael leaned over the counter, forehead pressed to his forearm.
"I know how it sounds. But that doesn't mean it's not real."

"This motherfucker is coming for me and I'm not ready!"

"Saying things like that isn't helping," Joseph said. "Calm down."

There was a beat of silence, and then Joseph said:

"Alright. Look. You know I've always been there for you."

Michael didn't respond.

"I mean it," Joseph said. "Remember that time in eighth grade? When those kids kept cornering you at the bus stop? You didn't tell anyone. You were gonna just let it keep happening."

Michael blinked. A flash of memory, muddy shoes, torn backpack straps, his brother stepping off his own bus early just to be there.

"You showed up outta nowhere," Michael said quietly. "Didn't even say anything. Just stood there."

"And they didn't bother you again, did they?" Joseph's voice had a firmness now.
"I've always been there."

Michael swallowed hard.
"I know."

"So I'm saying it again. Come out here. Stay with me and Lucy for a bit. Just long enough to breathe. Get your head straight. Start over."

Michael stayed silent.

"You don't owe anyone anything back there," Joseph added.
"Not anymore."

Michael stayed on the line, silent, staring at the chaos around him.

A chair with one leg snapped. The lamp still broken in the corner. The word *LINCOLN* staring back at him from the counter like a curse carved in stone.

He swallowed hard.

"I don't know what's happening to me, Joe," he said. "I used to be someone. I had a plan. I had control."

"You don't need control right now," Joseph replied. "You need space. Time. A reset."

Michael let the words hang there.

Outside, a car drove by slowly. Somewhere, a dog barked once and stopped. Everything felt oddly distant, like he was watching it all through the wrong end of a telescope.

"When would I leave?" he asked.

Joseph hesitated. "I could book you a flight. Get you out by tomorrow."

Michael shook his head, almost reflexively. "No. I'll drive."

"You sure?"

"Yeah," Michael said. "I need it. The road. The space. Just… putting miles between me and all this."

He looked around again, the overturned furniture, the shattered lamp, the inked word still screaming from the counter.

"Putting distance between me and Lincoln."

Joseph didn't answer right away. Then:

"Alright," he said. "The drive might be good for you. Might help clear your head."

Michael didn't reply. His mind was already halfway there, highways, gas stations, desert stretches where nothing looked back at you. Silence. Space.

Something about that felt right.

"I'll get the guest room ready," Joseph said. "You get here when you get here."

Michael nodded.

"I will."

They ended the call without goodbye.

Michael stood for a long moment, still holding the phone, thumb resting over the screen like he was afraid to let go.

Then he moved.

No rush, no panic. Just motion. Quiet, determined. He picked up a duffel bag from the closet, shook the dust out of it, and started to pack.

Not much. Just what he needed.

He left the mess as it was. He didn't clean. He didn't explain. There was nothing here that needed preserving.

Chapter 16: The Exodus

The house was still. Mangled blinds hung like broken ribs over the front window, filtering the morning light into warped stripes across the living room floor. Dust floated in the silence.

Michael stood in the doorway, duffel bag slung over one shoulder. A second-hand backpack hung low on the other. He took one last look at the room behind him, the wreckage left untouched since the break-in. Splintered chair legs. A coffee table with a fresh scar down the middle. The word *LINCOLN* still glaring from the counter like it had been burned into the laminate.

He didn't feel sorrow. Not quite. Just a hollow pull, like leaving the scene of an accident he'd caused but couldn't fully remember.

He locked the door behind him anyway, a strange formality for a man with nothing left worth stealing.

Out in the driveway, the Pinto wagon sat like a joke no one was brave enough to laugh at. Its fake wood paneling curled at the edges like paper caught in a flame. A dent in the rear quarter panel. Hubcaps mismatched, or missing. One of the taillights held in place with packing tape.

He walked slow, dragging the bags across the cracked concrete. No Italian loafers today. Flip-flops slapped against his heels, worn down from pacing inside a house that no longer felt like his.

He dropped his bags into the backseat with a thud and climbed in. The driver's seat let out a sigh under his weight. The air inside smelled like must and oil and something faintly metallic.

From the corner of his eye, movement.

Neighbors.

Across the street, Mrs. Dresden was standing by her mailbox in a pink robe, pretending to sort her mail. Two kids were crouched on the sidewalk with chalk, drawing smiling suns and crooked houses. A man walked his dog, slower than usual, watching Michael over the top of his sunglasses.

The whole cul-de-sac had stopped to witness the departure.

Michael leaned out the window and barked, "What the **fuck** are you looking at?"

Mrs. Dresden jumped. One of the kids dropped their chalk.

He twisted the key in the ignition. The Pinto coughed once. Twice. Then choked to life in a cloud of gray exhaust. It belched smoke into the summer air, right into the path of the chalk-art children. They waved it away, coughing.

Michael grinned.

"Yeah. That's what I thought."

He threw it in reverse. The transmission made a loud clunk. He didn't care. He backed into the street, the Pinto groaning the whole way, then jerked it into drive.

He didn't look back again. The Pinto rattled down the street, belching smoke and defiance.

Michael gripped the wheel with white knuckles, jaw clenched. The house, the job, the Range Rover, Kayla — all of it behind him. All of it poisoned.

All of it tied to one goddamn name.

He spat the words into the windshield like a curse. "Fuck you, Lincoln."

He slammed the window down, hot air rushing in.

"Keep the job. Keep the car. Keep Columbus. I'm done. I'm *gone*."

The Pinto surged forward in a cough of smoke, leaving the quiet little cul-de-sac and everything it stood for in a haze behind him.

Chapter 17: Land of Lincoln

The highway bent gently northeast, slicing through a corridor of fields the color of ash. He hadn't seen another car in fifteen minutes, just the endless groan of blacktop and the low buzz of wind slipping through a cracked window. His energy drink was warm. His knee ached. The air had that late-day thickness, like something was pressing down from above.

The sky looked tired.

He crested a slight rise and saw it:

A big green sign planted in the weeds like a warning label on a medication bottle.

"Welcome to Illinois – Land of Lincoln"

And right next to it, posted like a sneering sidekick:

"Tollway Ahead — $$"

He braked instinctively, though there was no reason. A cold prick of adrenaline slid up the back of his neck. He stared at the signs like they had spoken.

Lincoln.

That name again.

He gripped the steering wheel tighter, thumbs pressed into the leather. The skin on his knuckles went pale.

"Of course," he muttered. "Of course it's him."

The bile crept up without warning. Not anger, *offense*. The sheer *audacity* of that name meeting him at the border like some long-lost friend.

Land of Lincoln.

The words thudded around in his skull like a bad chorus. A state-sized shrine to the man whose ghost kept popping up like a virus in his life.

Every thread led back to that damn name.

And now, the state line was welcoming him into his personal hell with open arms and **two dollar signs.**

He laughed. A short, dry bark of disbelief.

"This Mother Fucker!" he said aloud, to no one. "What else do you want, Abe? You already ripped the girl away. Took the job. Burned down the house. Snatched the Range Rover out from under me. Was that not enough? Now I'm supposed to pay *you* just to drag my sorry ass through this endless cornfield wasteland you call a state?"

He spat the words out like venom, eyes burning into the cracked windshield as if Lincoln himself were lurking just beyond.

"That big man splitting rails with an ax—yeah, right. Or maybe it was chopping down some cherry tree? Who gives a damn? Some folk hero story to make you look noble while you bury the rest of us under your damn legacy."

He slammed his fist on the steering wheel so hard it jolted the car. The sound echoed inside like a gunshot in an empty room.

"Married that crazy-ass Mary Todd, didn't he? Goddamn whole state worshipping that deranged jagoff like he's carved out of pure granite or something."

He laughed, bitter and cracked, a dry rasp tearing through the silence.

"And now, here I am—paying toll after toll, lining your pockets while your ghost sneers from every goddamn signpost."

He shook his head, jaw clenched so tight his teeth ground together.

"I can almost *feel* your cold, bony fingers rifling through my pockets, hunting for my last goddamn nickel like some vulture circling the carcass of my life."

He leaned closer to the steering wheel, voice dropping to a harsh whisper.

"And all for what? The privilege to rattle over these cracked, raggedy roads through this rotting carcass of a place—Midwestern decay, rust and regret bleeding out with every goddamn mile I drive."

The sign loomed behind him now, disappearing into the dust kicked up by his back tires. But the words still echoed, as if they'd been branded into the rearview.

Land of Lincoln.

A whole goddamn state.

He looked around, cracked highway, dead trees, a field of rusted equipment sitting like forgotten gods, and it hit him:

This wasn't a land. It was a *trap*. A monument to loss. A footnote to someone else's legacy, paved over with toll lanes and gas stations that smelled like old hot dogs.

He glanced down. Gas tank at a quarter. Wallet thinner than a communion wafer.

He clenched his jaw.

He could feel the weight of that name like a hand on

his back, cold and unrelenting, pushing him forward into whatever came next.

And somewhere, he imagined, Lincoln was smiling. Not a warm, statesmanlike smile. Not the gentle, grandfatherly benevolence from the history books. No, this was something thinner. Drier. Almost smug. Like a man who'd already read the ending and knew how badly it all went for you.

That name.

Lincoln.

It clung to his life like black mold, growing in quiet corners, feeding on loss, popping up again just when he thought he'd finally scrubbed it away.

It wasn't just a coincidence anymore.

It was a gravity. A pressure on the chest.

Not a person, but a *presence*.

He could feel it sitting behind his ribs.

In the hollow place where hope used to live.

"Land of Lincoln," he whispered, voice dry and cracked. "Like he owns the goddamn air now."

He turned the AC off and cracked the window wider, as if that would ease the weight, but it didn't. It stayed with him. Like the lingering memory of a conversation that went too far. Like the silence after a slammed door.

Somewhere behind the green sign, Illinois sprawled out like a bad decision.

Flat. Grey. Toll-plagued.

An entire stretch of landscape carpeted in *him*.

Lincoln on the road signs.

Lincoln on the license plates.

Lincoln in the courthouse names and the gas stations and the goddamn *library cards*.

He felt like a man walking willingly into the open jaws of the beast that had already chewed him up once and spat him out in pieces.

And the worst part?

No one else seemed to notice.

To everyone else, it was just a sign. Just a name. Just a state.

But not to him.

To him, it was the entrance to a living mausoleum built in the image of a man who wouldn't leave him the hell alone.

A temple of asphalt and bureaucracy.

And at its center, somewhere far ahead, was the same solemn, towering face… waiting.

He shifted in his seat. His hands were slick on the wheel.

He hadn't even reached the tollbooth yet.

His fists unclenched slowly, fingers tracing invisible patterns on the steering wheel.

He leaned back in his seat, the tight knot of rage loosening just a fraction.

"Fuck it," he muttered, voice low and rough. "It is what it is."

The engine hummed steadily beneath him, a steady pulse in the quiet cab of the car.

Outside, the fields stretched on, dry, endless, and indifferent. The sky burned high and empty above.

He let out a slow breath, trying to wrestle some peace from the chaos clawing inside his head.

But he knew it wouldn't last long.

Ahead, the toll booth loomed like a sentinel in his path, the next stop on this godforsaken highway of Lincoln's making.

He could already feel the old anger stirring back to life, like a storm waiting just beyond the horizon.

The slow crawl toward the toll, the clinking coins, the sharp sting of the transaction, each one a little barb, a reminder that this nightmare wasn't over yet.

He straightened, fingers tightening on the wheel once more.

Ready or not, here it comes.

The road narrowed.

Lanes funneled inward like a cattle chute, channeling him toward the inevitable. Ahead, the tollbooth sat hunched on the horizon like a gray little fortress, low, square, faceless. Fluorescent lights buzzed overhead in defiance of the daylight, casting a cold, jaundiced glow across the concrete.

He slowed, foot easing off the gas as the line of cars ahead thickened, five, maybe six of them, all inching forward like prisoners toward processing. The booth windows blinked. Red lights. Green lights. A mechanical rhythm, empty and brutal.

And above it all, just in case he'd forgotten for a single second:

ILLINOIS TOLLWAY – LAND OF LINCOLN

There it was. One more time. One more fucking time.

"Of course," he whispered. "Still watching. Still collecting."

The sign looked down on him like the face of a smiling tax collector from the 1800s. A toll to cross your own country. A price tag to enter your own failure.

The GPS chirped, perky as ever:

"Keep right in point two miles for toll plaza."

He reached out and shut the voice off mid-sentence.

He didn't need a machine to tell him he was headed into the meat grinder.

The line crept forward. He tapped the wheel. Tapped again. The same six inches of movement, over and over.

He could hear the *clink* of coins from the car ahead. The low murmur of someone arguing with the toll booth operator. A receipt flapping in the wind like a taunt.

He rubbed his temples. Sweat gathered at his collar, made worse by the stagnant air and heat radiating up from the asphalt.

He thought about turning around. Briefly. But there was no exit. No alternate path.

Just the booth, the bar, the dollar sign, and the invisible hand of Lincoln stretching out once more.

As his car inched closer, he could see the toll collector now. A tired man in a neon vest, half-asleep, handing out change without looking anyone in the eye. No smile. No greeting. A human postage stamp.

The driver in the lane beside him, a man in a sun-bleached Toyota, was fumbling with a crumpled five-dollar bill. It floated out the window. He watched it drift in the air, then tumble under another car's tire. Gone.

"Jesus," he muttered. "It's a goddamn feeding trough."

Three cars ahead now.

He dug into his glove box. A fistful of change, sticky, hot, and metallic. He counted silently, lips barely moving.

The car ahead pulled off.

Two more.

His breathing got shallow. His left eye twitched.

Don't say anything, he told himself. *Just pay. Just go.*

But it was too late. He could already feel it building again. The fury. The itch under his skin. The pounding in his temples like someone knocking to be let out.

The sign above him flashed red. WAIT.

The bar stayed down. Just long enough to feel personal.

The booth loomed now. Two cars left.

The sun caught the windshield just right, blinding him for half a second. He winced, reached for the visor, but it was already gone. Just the afterimage of that red sign burned onto his retinas.

WAIT.

"Yeah," he muttered. "That's the story of my life."

The car in front of him wasn't moving. He watched the driver's hand stick out the window, fluttering like an old moth, holding what looked like a twenty-dollar bill.

He leaned slightly to the left, trying to see the toll worker's face. Nothing. Just a slumped shadow behind glass, like a mannequin in a DMV diorama. A cardboard cutout with a pulse.

Time crawled. The wind outside had gone still, the air inside his car thick.

He looked at the dashboard clock.

It hadn't moved.

He exhaled like he'd just been holding his breath for hours.

The smell of hot plastic and old receipts filled the cab. A sun-warped takeout bag was wedged between the seat and center console, he didn't even remember what it was from.

Still one car ahead. Still stuck.

He glanced to his right.

In the next lane, a family SUV had rolled down its window. A kid in the backseat was staring straight at him, nursing a juice box straw like it was a religious experience. The mother was on her phone. The father looked dead behind the eyes.

The kid waved. Slowly. Creepily. Like a ghost in a found-footage movie.

He looked away.

The radio sparked back to life for half a second, just static and the last syllable of a commercial.
He slapped it off.

Clink.

Another coin hit the metal tray in the next lane.

He looked down at his own handful of change. Clammy. Mismatched. He'd run out of quarters. How the hell had he run out of quarters?

He sifted through nickels and dimes like he was counting out a ransom.

The car ahead of him finally started to move. The brake lights flared. The gate lifted.

Now it was his turn.

WAIT, the red sign said again.

Of course.

He rolled forward slowly. The metal railing to his left shimmered like a mirage. One bump of the wheel and it'd scrape.

The car stopped. Brakes hissed. Engine ticking.

The tollbooth stared back at him like a bad joke, squat, gray, buzzing under cheap lights, its window smeared with dead bugs and human fingerprints.

Inside, the attendant sat like a taxidermy experiment. Eyes glazed. Soul departed.

He leaned out the window, sweaty coins in hand, a pathetic cocktail of nickels, dimes, and a healthy scatter of pennies. Dozens of little Lincolns. All of them grinning that tight-lipped martyr smirk.

Clink. Clink. Clink.

The man behind the glass peered at the coins.

Flat voice:

"Sorry, sir. We don't accept pennies."

Time stopped.

He blinked once.

"Excuse me?"

"No pennies."

A pause.

He looked down at the copper in his palm. Lincoln stared up at him with a shit-eating grin, like he'd been waiting for this moment since the day he posed for the bust. Like he knew something. Like he'd always known.

Michael held one up to the light. Just one.

"Are you serious right now?" he said, tone rising. "You're telling me... in the *Land of Lincoln*... the place that slapped his name on every sign, every road, every rest stop toilet... you don't accept his currency?"

The booth worker shrugged.

That was it.

That was the last match.

He barked a laugh, not amused, not even angry. Something *else*. Something frayed and gurgling.

"Oh wow. Oh that's rich."

He held up another penny, then another. Lincoln, Lincoln, Lincoln.

"You see these? You see this smug motherfucker?"

He jabbed the penny at the glass.

"He took my job. My girl. My goddamn *car*. Now he's taking *this*, too? This?!" He shook the handful of change like a threat.

"I'm supposed to pay to enter this cornfield nightmare with a smile on my face and a Lincoln in my hand, and suddenly, he's not good enough?"

He was nearly shouting now, leaning half out of the window, wind catching the sweat on his brow.

"You don't take Lincoln anymore. That's rich. That's poetic. That's fucking biblical!"

A driver in the next lane was staring now. Mouth half-open.

The toll worker had stopped blinking.

He wasn't done.

"You know what? Good. Maybe it's time you rejected him. Maybe the whole country should. Big man, rail-splitting, stovepipe-wearing *fantasy*. Oh, he freed the slaves, and now he's here to shiv me for *thirty-five cents* at the edge of his failed wasteland empire."

He held up the penny again, two fingers pinching it like something diseased.

"Look at him. Look at that beady-eyed messiah. This is who we put on money? The man who married a lunatic, grew a neckbeard, and made Illinois his little kingdom of broken highways, moral superiority and political corruption?"

No response.

Just the hum of the booth fan and the distant *clink* of someone else's payment being accepted.

He leaned forward slowly. Pressed the penny, Lincoln's copper face first, against the tollbooth glass. Pressed it hard. Until his knuckles went white.

The booth worker flinched, just slightly.

His voice dropped. Calm now. Too calm.

"You're his now," he whispered. "You live in his house. You take his name. You tell people what you *won't* take, but you took that uniform. That air. That silence."

He peeled the penny from the glass, leaving a faint round smear of sweat and skin oil. A ghost print. A copper stain.

He dropped it on the tray. Just one. Just that one.

Then sat back.

And waited.

The toll worker didn't move at first.

Just stared at the tray. At the single penny lying there like evidence in a crime scene.
A dirty copper disc. One eye worn flat. Lincoln's busted little smirk staring up from a smudge of grime and sweat.

The man blinked. Once. Twice.

Then, without a word, he reached for the manual override.
The gate lifted.

No receipt. No farewell. Just the red and white striped arm rising like a reluctant blessing.

He didn't say thank you. Didn't look back. Just dropped the car into gear and rolled forward, slow and steady, like something sacred had just been violated.

The tires thumped over the seam in the pavement. The booth disappeared in his periphery.

But in the mirror, it remained.

That little square of glass, flickering behind him, still held the faint round mark where the penny had pressed. A perfect greasy halo.

And the booth worker?

Still staring.

Still not moving.

Just a man behind glass, held hostage by a coin and a meltdown he hadn't been trained for.

He didn't drive fast. He let the engine pull him forward, as if even the car wanted to get away from whatever had just happened.

The road curved west, dull and flat and endless. Cornfields. Billboards. A whole horizon of things he didn't care about.

But for a moment, before the booth faded completely behind the rise, he saw it again in the mirror.

He didn't turn the radio on.
Didn't speak.
Didn't curse or breathe heavy or try to make sense of any of it.

He just drove.

The road unfolded in slow, lazy lines. Cracked blacktop. Faded stripes. Fields stretching out on both sides like some kind of prison yard that forgot to end.

The sun was starting its descent, dipping low and harsh, turning the windshield into molten glass. He didn't adjust the visor. Let it burn. Let it smear his vision in streaks of gold and blood-orange.

The tires hummed.

The engine murmured.

And inside, nothing.

Not calm. Not peace. Just a blank space where adrenaline had been.

A weightless pocket.

His hands were tight on the wheel, knuckles pale.

He noticed, flexed them. Didn't ease up.

The air in the car felt thick and mixed with manure and smog from outside.

No traffic ahead.

None behind.

Just him.

The road.

The hum.

And somewhere, out of sight, but not out of mind, a tollbooth with a single greasy ghost print, and a penny left behind like a curse.

Chapter 18: Purgatory of the Plains

The motel bed felt like it had been dredged from a basement—damp underneath, too soft in the middle, too hard at the edges. Sleep hadn't happened. Just a long stretch of staring at the ceiling, counting cracks and trying not to think.

By 4:00 a.m., he was gone.

The air outside was thick and still. No wind, no movement, just the hum of the highway a few blocks away and the buzz of the vacancy sign flickering behind him. He didn't look back.

The Pinto shuddered awake on the third try. He tapped the dash like it might help—habit, not hope. The headlights smeared a dull path through the darkness as he pulled out of the gravel lot, tires crunching the gravel beneath the rubber.

He headed west. The road opened in front of him, wide and empty, the kind of dark that eats headlights. A few semi-trucks passed in the other lane, distant and slow, hauling whatever still needed hauling at this hour. He drove on.

As the horizon began to shift, faint blue leaking into the black, he passed the sleeping edge of Omaha. Strip malls, gas stations, shuttered chain restaurants blurred by.

He sighed, eyes dropping to the gas gauge. Just over a quarter tank.

"I'll need to stop soon."

Reaching for his phone, he typed "gas station" into the GPS.

A tap later, the screen lit up: nearest gas, Lincoln, Nebraska. He stared at it. Blinked once. Then laughed, short and mean.

"Aw hell no!"

The dashboard glowed faintly in the dark cab. "Yeah, of course. Of *course* it's there. Where else would it be? Right in the heart of the Prairie's Purgatory, dedicated to the Patron Saint of Sanctimonious Bullshit."

"No fucking way I'm stopping there," he muttered, shaking his head. "Not today. Not ever."

He could feel it already, just seeing the name on the screen—*Lincoln*—like an infected splinter under his skin. That name had started to rot everything.

"Son of a bitch has his own damn city now," he said to no one. "Whole fucking town named after him.

He slapped the steering wheel.

"Saint Abe. Bearded messiah of mediocrity." "Fuck You!" He barked out.

His voice was rising. Bitter. Cracked. "The whole world paying homage to this emaciated, hollow eyed, scarecrow."

The Pinto groaned under the strain as he floored it past the exit sign.

Green letters. White reflective glow. **LINCOLN – 1 MILE.**

"Fuck you, Lincoln" he hissed, eyes burning. "I'd rather push this car through a minefield than stop in your precious little shrine."

He watched the exits slide by in the mirror, small, dark, and silent.

He pushed the pedal harder, desperate to leave town in his rear-view mirror.

"Keep your gas," he muttered. "Keep your streets and your statues and your goddamn ghost. I'll burn before I kneel."

Chapter 19: Gas Station in Purgatory

About an hour past Lincoln, the cracked highway stretched out in front of him, a narrow ribbon slicing through the endless sea of cornfields. He pulled the Pinto off the cracked highway and eased into the gas station next to pump 3, a flickering beacon swallowed by a sea of endless cornfields. The sky was heavy, swollen with humidity that clung to everything like a damp shroud.

Stepping out, the heat hit him like a fist wrapped in wet burlap. Around the streetlights, huge halos shimmered and pulsed, ghostly rings bending the moist air into soft, blurry circles that seemed to hover just beyond reach. It was that kind of oppressive humidity that pressed against your skin, settled in your lungs, and filled your nostrils with a thick, sour tang.

The faint but unmistakable stench of manure drifted on the breeze, slow and pungent, an invisible reminder that the sprawling cornfields were alive with their own rot and decay.

The silence of the early morning pulsed with the low, relentless hum of insects, not a sound, but a presence. A vibration in the air. They moved as one, a sentient swarm, thick with intent. A crawling cloud of biblical pestilence, torn from a fevered chapter of Revelation, stretching from ditch to sky

Then something larger landed on his shirt, a golf ball-sized monstrosity, its shell crusty and cracked like old leather, mottled brown and black. His fingers instinctively reached to brush it off, but the creature's hooked claws snagged in the fabric, holding fast like the tenacious grip of Velcro.

He tugged hard, the bug clinging stubbornly, its weight dragging his shirt down. With a sharp, frustrated jerk, he tore it free and backhanded it into the gravel, watching it skitter away. A shudder ran through him, disgust and unease curling in his gut.

He wiped his palm on his jeans, a sudden prickling unease crawling up his spine.

With a grunt, he pushed open the gas station door, stepping into a stale cloud of smoke and sweat. The fluorescent lights flickered overhead, buzzing softly like a swarm of angry bees trapped inside a plastic box. The air was thick, heavy with nicotine and damp, like the inside of an old lung.

Behind the counter stood the clerk, skinny and hunched, almost swallowed by a battered shirt that hung off his frame like a second skin. His face was pale, eyes sunken deep beneath dark, tired lids. He didn't even glance up as the door creaked open. Instead, he took a long drag from his cigarette, smoke curling around his fingers like some poisonous serpent.

Then the cough came, a harsh, rattling bark that shook his shoulders and echoed in the small room. It wasn't a cough that cleared the throat; it was a machine grinding rust, a wheeze soaked in years of bad decisions. He coughed until he nearly doubled over, the sound rough and raw, then stopped abruptly to spit into a grimy sink behind the counter.

Without looking up, the clerk rasped, "Thirty dollars. Pump three."

The words were flat, mechanical, like a broken record stuck on repeat. Then, without another glance, he slid back into his haze of smoke and coughs, the grim soundtrack for the island of isolated despair.

As the clerk slide the bills into the register, his eyes lingered for a fraction longer on the cracked tiles beneath the clerk's feet, the stains and scuffs telling stories he didn't want to hear.

He stepped back outside, the door creaking shut behind him, sealing the stench and misery inside. The humid, breaking dawn waited, thick and unforgiving, as he took a deep breath and returned to the Pinto.

Chapter 20: Cheyenne

He pulled off the highway earlier than usual, the sun hanging stubbornly high in the sky. Cheyenne stretched out before him, a patchwork of faded storefronts and cracked sidewalks shimmering under the unforgiving afternoon light.

He hadn't planned to stop here, but something in his body screamed for a break. Maybe it was the gnawing exhaustion. Maybe just the hollow quiet behind his eyes.

He cruised slowly through downtown, where the streets were sparsely populated, just a handful of people moving languidly through the heat, heads down, shadows clinging to the edges of buildings. Street lamps buzzed faintly even in daylight, their filaments rattling like they'd forgotten how to sleep. The air was dry. The heat baked the chipped paint and rusted fire escapes.

The motel caught his eye, a weathered, squat building squinting under the sun, its faded sign announcing *Vacancy* in cracked, peeling letters. It looked like it hadn't changed since the Reagan administration.

The parking lot was cracked and dusty, litter scattered like dead leaves. A flickering bulb buzzed weakly over the office door.

He parked without care.

Inside the office, the smell hit him first, a stale mix of old smoke, cheap air freshener, and the sharp tang of baked in mildew. It clung to the walls, thick enough to chew. The clerk barely glanced up, her eyes shadowed beneath tired lids, a cigarette smoldering at her fingertips.

"Thirty-five cash or card," she said flatly, sliding a key across the counter without a smile.

He dug out bills, counting slowly, the weight of the day sinking deeper.

The hallway to his room was narrow and lit by harsh fluorescent strips, the carpet threadbare and stained.

He stepped inside. The room was sterile in the bright daylight, no shadows to hide the peeling wallpaper, the ancient TV perched crooked on the dresser, or the threadbare bedspread that looked like it had witnessed every kind of misery.

He dropped his bag, his fingers lingering on the edge of the mattress.

Outside the window, the city sprawled beneath the relentless sun, indifferent and unyielding.

He lay back on the bed without meaning to, the mattress groaning beneath him. For a while, he just stared at the ceiling, letting the silence settle in, heavy and stale. But the quiet wasn't comforting, it only made the noise in his head louder. After a few minutes, maybe more, he peeled himself up, splashed cold water on his face in the cracked bathroom mirror, and stood there watching the droplets slide off his chin. The day was still too bright. Too long. He needed something to take the edge off, something to drown out the drone of his own thoughts. He grabbed his wallet—what little was left of it—and stepped out into the street. The motel door clicked shut behind him. A few blocks later, he found a place.

Outside, a rusted Miller High Life sign hung crooked, its faded slogan, "The Champagne of Beers"—hanging like a ghost from better days. He pushed open the door; from the darkness came a wave of stale air that hit him hard, thick with sweat, spilled beer, and the tang in the exhale of a mop that died trying.

The door protested loudly on its rusted hinges as he pushed inside, the sudden shift from hot highway sun to dim, stale shade hitting him like a slap. The air inside was thick.

He planted his boots on the threadbare carpet that clung like a damp rag to the floor, its dull reddish-brown surface mottled with countless dark stains, each one a mystery of what had been dropped or spilled and forgotten. The fabric was grimy underfoot, slightly tacky in places, stubbornly holding onto the grime of years past.

The room was lit by flickering neon signs advertising long-forgotten brands of beer, buzzing softly and casting an uneven glow that made the peeling wallpaper look like it was melting. A single bare bulb dangled over the bar, buzzing faintly, its dim light flickering like a dying pulse.

In the corner, the jukebox blinked and sputtered before spitting out a slow country tune with a voice gravelly and strained, as if the singer was singing through a mouthful of dust. The guitar strummed a tired, aching melody that seeped into the silence, setting the tone like an old wound freshly uncovered.

Around the bar, a handful of men slouched with the air of permanent fatigue. They wore weathered flannel shirts with frayed cuffs, stained denim, and faces carved from long winters and harder luck. One man absentmindedly rolled a cigarette, his fingers stained yellow and cracked, his eyes flickering to the door then away, wary but resigned.

Then there was her. She sat alone near the back; a tower of defiant hair sculpted into a beehive that refused to acknowledge the last five decades. The towering structure of dark hair looked out of place here—a misplaced relic daring to survive among peeling paint and rusted beer taps. Her lips curled into a knowing smirk as her eyes met his across the room.

The floor creaked softly beneath shifting bodies, and the occasional scrape of a chair added a rhythm to the murmur of quiet conversations and clinking bottles.

He slid onto a cracked vinyl stool at the bar, its torn leather exposing yellowed foam beneath, sticky and reluctant to give way. The bartender, a stoic figure marked by a scar slicing through a graying beard, nodded silently and wiped down a glass with a rag that looked as old as the bar itself.

The jukebox switched to a raspier voice, the melancholy of the song pulling at the edges of his frayed patience, mixing with the dull ache of exhaustion curling low in his chest. For the first time in days, he let the music press against him like a dark comfort, strange and unwelcome but needed all the same.

The woman with the impossible hair caught his eye again, a brief, almost imperceptible smile curling at the corner of her mouth. The world outside, the cracked highways, the relentless sun—felt miles away. Here, in this grimy bar, amid the sticky carpet and peeling wallpaper, something fragile was beginning to flicker.

A couple drinks in, the edges of everything started to smooth out.

The musty smell of the place no longer curled his stomach. His nose had adjusted, or maybe he just didn't care anymore. The carpet didn't stick quite so much under his boots. Or if it did, he didn't notice. The warped country twang rolling out of the jukebox had shifted from grating to strangely tolerable, even comforting in a low, drunken kind of way. It reminded him of something, not a memory, exactly, but a feeling from some distant part of life where things were still held together.

The ache behind his eyes had dulled to a steady throb. The tension in his shoulders started to let go. His brain, for once, wasn't trying to claw out of his skull. He slouched forward on the bar, ran a thumb along the lip of his bottle, and caught himself... humming. Barely. Almost too low to notice. But still.

He took a slow look around.

The rednecks had faded into the background. No one here gave a shit about who he was or where he came from. He wasn't the guy who lost the girl, the house, the job, the car. He was just a guy on a barstool at 3:15 in the afternoon, half-drunk and finally still for once.

And across the room, she was still there.

Ms. Beehive.

A full can of Aqua Net's worth of defiance wrapped around a fading kind of glamour.

She was sipping whiskey from a short glass, elbow resting on the table, long nails tapping absently along its rim. Their eyes met again. This time, the glance lingered.

She didn't smile. Not quite. But the corners of her mouth shifted. Something between curiosity and challenge.

He glanced down at his beer, considered it like it held the answer. Then flagged the bartender.

"What's she drinking?"

The bartender didn't look up from his glass polishing. "Old Crow."

Of course she was.

He slid a few crumpled bills across the bar. "Send her another."

The bartender didn't say a word. Just nodded once, poured the amber liquid into a fresh glass, and delivered it with the kind of ceremony reserved for strangers who drink alone too often.

She looked at the glass, then over at him.

Lifted it slightly in a silent toast.

He raised his own drink in response.

The next song on the jukebox kicked in, something with a slow, slinky groove and a steel guitar that sounded like it was flirting with regret. Not romantic, not happy. But it had a pulse.

Things didn't feel good exactly. But they didn't feel doomed either.

And after the week he'd had, that counted for something.

She settled onto the stool beside him with a sigh and a creak of cracked vinyl, set her drink down, and turned her body toward his like they'd been mid-conversation all along.

"You always this generous to strangers in strange places?" she asked, voice low and husky. Not sexy in a practiced way—more like cigarette smoke and gravel roads. It fit her perfectly.

He shrugged. "Only when they look like they might have a good story."

That got a small smile out of her, subtle, a little crooked. The kind of smile that doesn't ask permission.

"Maybe I do," she said. "Or maybe I'm just thirsty."

He glanced at her drink. "I figured a second round might loosen one or the other."

Up close, her beehive was even more absurd. A towering black helmet of teased and sprayed hair that defied physics, time, and good judgment. But her eyes... they were sharp. Alert. A little bloodshot, maybe, but watching everything.

She took another sip, then nodded toward his nearly empty bottle.

"You drinking that out of habit, or preference?"

He looked down. "At this point, I'm not sure there's a difference."

"Let me pick the next round," she said, raising two fingers toward the bartender. "Two whiskeys. Make 'em full pours."

He raised an eyebrow but didn't stop her. Whiskey wasn't what he'd started the day with, but she seemed to know what she wanted.

"You don't even know if I can handle that."

She smirked. "You look like a man who's survived worse."

The bartender returned with two glasses of something dark and strong. She pushed one toward him and lifted hers.

"To surviving worse," she said.

They clinked glasses.

The whiskey hit like a shot to the ribs, clean, fast, and just mean enough to feel honest.

No names exchanged. No unnecessary words. Just two drifters at the edge of something, sharing a table in a half-dead bar.

And for a moment, he didn't feel quite as lost.

She excused herself with a touch on his arm, the barest graze of skin on fabric, and slipped off the barstool. Her boots clicked down the length of the bar toward the restrooms. He watched her go—not leering, just observing. She walked like someone who'd been knocked down a few times and didn't much care what anyone thought anymore. He respected that.

Then it was just him. Alone again, but not lonely. Not tonight.

He took a slow pull of the whiskey she'd ordered. It was a little cheap, a little mean—but it warmed his ribs and smoothed out the ragged noise that had been dragging around inside him for weeks.

He looked around at the dim corners of the bar, the sagging booths, the jukebox leaking steel guitar into the low haze of afternoon light. Still daylight out. Still early by the old rules. Once, not that long ago, he'd never have touched a drink before dark. Had rules. Structure. Shit to do.

And now here he was, day-drinking with bustouts.

He half-smiled at the thought. Not cruel, not self-pitying. Just... honest. The sort of honesty that only comes when you stop pretending you're better than where you ended up.

It wasn't joy, not even close. But it was that strange, hard-earned quiet. The kind that settles into you when you *surrender to the shape of your life*—even if that shape looks nothing like the one you planned. When the fight drains out of your arms and you stop trying to fix it all. Just sit with it. Let it be wrecked.

And in that surrender, there was a sliver of peace, fragile, but real. Like a quiet harbor after a long storm. Not redemption. Not happiness. Just calm. The kind of calm you find when you stop clawing against the tide and let it carry you, at least for a while.

There was no one here to perform for. No inbox. No cold calls. No one who remembered who he used to be or gave a shit about who he might've been. Just the sour stink of spilled beer and the low pulse of a jukebox stuck in heartbreak mode. And her.

He caught a glimpse of himself in the mirror behind the bar. Eyes bloodshot, collar rumpled, skin dull from too many nights without sleep.

But he looked... fine. Not *good*, but fine. Alive. And maybe, for the first time in a long while, not completely lost.

Across the street was his motel, waiting. The kind of place where they didn't ask questions or clean too well, but right now it felt like the Ritz. He wasn't planning tomorrow. He wasn't thinking about yesterday. He was just letting the moment breathe.

The jukebox kicked into another song. Something slower. Sadder. He didn't mind.

Things, God help him, might actually be starting to look up.

She nudged him gently, fingers brushing his arm, sending a faint jolt through the dull fog in his mind. Her eyes flicked around the bar like she was weighing the place up for the last time.

"You got a place to crash, or am I gonna have to start scouting the alleyways?" she asked, a half-smile tugging at her lips.

He rubbed the back of his neck, a little embarrassed. "Yeah, I got a room across the street. Nothing fancy, just a dump, really. Motel 6 style."

She chuckled, the sound low and surprisingly warm. "Sounds perfect. Let's get the hell out of here before this place starts smelling worse."

They pushed through the door together and into the hazy afternoon light. The sun hung low but still strong, casting long shadows across cracked sidewalks and faded storefronts.

Around them, the street was coming alive with early evening traffic, commuters in tired suits, a mom juggling groceries and a screaming kid, a few teenagers blasting music from an old pickup truck. The city was moving on, oblivious to the haze clinging to them.

A group of suited men brushed past, briefcases in hand, faces tight with deadlines and day-old fatigue. He noticed their quick glances—half curiosity, half judgment—as if they could smell the cheap whiskey clinging to his skin.

He felt the weight of their world pressing down: responsible, ordered, the kind of life he used to have, or thought he did.

She walked beside him, easy and unbothered, humming softly to the faint country tune drifting from a nearby car.

Despite the noise and movement, there was a strange peace in the aimless wandering. The sticky bar and the sharp burn of whiskey were already fading into something softer, more forgiving.

They crossed the street together, the neon sign of the motel flickering in the daylight like a tired beacon, half inviting, half warning.

Inside the cramped room, he closed the door behind them, the click echoing like a final punctuation.

For a moment, silence settled heavy and thick, pressing in from the cracked windows and peeling wallpaper.

He sank onto the bed, the thin mattress groaning under him.

Maybe this, this quiet surrender, was what he needed. Not peace exactly, but a pause. A breath.

Back in the motel room, the air hung thick and sour, like years of sweat and sorrow had soaked into the faded wallpaper and never left.

The ceiling light flickered faintly, casting slow-moving shadows that made the cracks in the walls feel deeper than they were.

The old air conditioner buzzed in the corner, more suggestion than relief.

From the chipped porcelain sink, he retrieved two beers from the ice bucket.

The bottles were sweating, their necks slick with condensation that dripped and pooled on the scarred dresser.

She lingered by the bed, the dim light catching the subtle shimmer in her eyes. Her posture was casual, legs crossed at the knee, but there was a quiet calculation in the way she watched him, a predator patient before the strike.

They raised their bottles, clinking softly, the sound oddly intimate in the oppressive quiet. He took a long drink, letting the bitter liquid wash down the raw edges of his nerves, the cold sting a fleeting relief.

As he settled onto the threadbare edge of the mattress, a strange calm began to settle over him, as if the dark corners of his day were folding inward, momentarily softened by the numbness spreading through his limbs.

But then the pressure in his gut pulled him toward the bathroom. He set his beer carefully on the edge of the dresser, just beside the cracked mirror streaked with grime and cigarette smoke residue. The bottle trembled slightly, forgotten.

"I'll be right back," he murmured, more to himself than to her.

He stepped into the cramped bathroom, the door creaking as he closed it behind him. The musty scent of mildew wrapped around him, the cracked tiles cold beneath his feet.

Inside, he stared into his own tired eyes in the mirror, tracing the dark circles and scratches of sleepless nights, the deep lines etched in the corners of his mouth that refused to relax. He rubbed his temples, desperate to clear the fog thickening his thoughts.

Meanwhile, outside the bathroom, the room was silent but for the faint drip of condensation.

She rose slowly, moving toward the dresser with the ease of someone who's done this before, every gesture smooth and precise.

From her pocket, she pulled a tiny foil packet, fingertips flicking it open without a sound.

A single pill, no bigger than a Tic Tac, slid from the packet and dropped into the forgotten beer.

The pill disappeared beneath the golden surface, a small ripple the only sign of its presence.

She paused a moment, watching the bubbles rise lazily, then glanced toward the bathroom door, a faint, almost amused smile touching her lips.

Back inside, he took a last breath, washed his face, then turned toward the door, unaware that the moment he stepped back into the room, the world was about to tilt beneath him.

He stepped back into the cramped motel room, the stale smell of cheap carpet and old cigarettes pressing in around him. His beer sat on the scratched dresser, sweating in the dim afternoon light that streamed through the wide-open curtains. Without hesitation, he grabbed the bottle and brought it to his lips, swallowing the last bitter gulp in one long, ragged pull.

The cold liquid burned a path down his throat, sharp and unwelcome, but he didn't care. His hands moved almost on their own, fumbling at the buttons of his shirt, each one popping free slowly as the weight of exhaustion pressed down on him.

"Hey," he said, voice rough, low with fatigue, "can you close the curtains?"

The fabric hung limp, the room still flooded with the dull, fading daylight. But she didn't move. Her eyes met his briefly, a flicker of something unreadable there, then she looked away.

He blinked, squinting against the glare, his fingers trembling as they wrestled with the stubborn buttons. The edges of his vision blurred, colors melting into one another like paint bleeding on a wet canvas.

A dull throb started behind his temples, steady and unrelenting, as the room began to tilt. His balance faltered, knees buckling just slightly. The world shifted, becoming softer, slower.

He blinked hard again, but the dizziness only deepened, wrapping around him like a tightening noose. His shirt hung open now, exposing skin that felt suddenly cold, vulnerable.

The curtains remained wide, the harsh light slicing into the room without mercy.

His breath caught, heart pounding in slow, heavy beats.

And then the edges of everything frayed, unraveling into black.

He collapsed backward, the world tilting beneath him, and the last thing he felt was the grimy motel carpet scraping against his skin as darkness swallowed him whole.

Whether it had been seconds or hours, he couldn't tell. He came to in fragments, slow, disjointed, like someone reassembling reality from the scattered pieces of a dream.

His head throbbed. Not just pain, pressure. A deep, pulsing ache that bloomed behind his eyes and pushed outward like something trying to claw its way free from inside his skull.

His mouth was dry. Not just thirsty, arid. Tongue thick as rope, lips stuck together. Breathing through his nose didn't help; a faintly metallic, chemical taste lingered in his mouth. His skin felt tight, damp with sweat gone cold.

The ceiling above him hovered in and out of focus, the cracks in the plaster swimming lazily like lines on water. For a moment, it all felt like a dream. A strange, heavy dream he hadn't quite exited yet. Everything was too slow. Too soft. Too far away.

He blinked. Once. Twice. Then the room breathed.

A glow washed over the ceiling, red, seeping in from the window. Not warm red. Not firelight. This was chemical, unnatural. A fluorescent, blood-orange pulse that bathed the entire ceiling in sick light. Then it dimmed. Gone. Then, again, brighter this time. Then gone. Like a slow, demonic heartbeat.

He turned his head, every movement cutting like glass behind his eyes. The room was empty. The chair she'd sat in was tipped slightly away from the table. His beer bottle was empty.

The curtains were still open.

He stared at them, and the glow came again, this time flooding the room in its full force. The walls lit up like they were burning from the inside. The carpet, the dresser, even his skin, all painted in that pulsing, radioactive red.

And then, black.

He lay there, still, as it cycled again. Bright. Blinding. Then gone.

The rhythm of it matched the pounding in his skull. Perfectly synchronized. Like it was inside him. Like the light and the pain were connected. A shared frequency.

He closed his eyes, but the red burned through his lids, imprinting itself into his brain.

The realization came slowly. Like puzzle pieces rearranging themselves behind his eyes. The bar. The woman. The drink. Her laugh, distant now, like it had happened to someone else. He'd gone to the bathroom. Left his beer on the table.

And then, nothing.

His hand moved instinctively to his back pocket. Empty.

A jolt of clarity cut through the haze. He pushed himself to the side, searching the floor. There, his wallet. Facedown near the corner of the bed, splayed open like a wound. Credit cards scattered across the dirty carpet like dropped playing cards.

The cash—gone.

All of it.

Even the singles.

He stared at the empty billfold, trying to process the quiet violence of it. It felt obscene, surgical, almost. Not just stolen. Stripped. She hadn't just taken his money; she'd peeled off a layer of whatever dignity he had left.

His stomach turned.

He tried to sit up, the room tilting sideways like a boat on rough water. He made it to his knees, crawling, then bracing himself against the edge of the window.

He looked out.

The glass was dirty, smudged with fingerprints and time, but the light outside was too violent to ignore. It slammed through the pane in flashes, blood-red, sickly pink, almost ultraviolet, cutting the night into stuttering fragments. The air itself seemed to throb with each pulse.

Across the street: **LINCOLN LIQUORS**.

The sign wasn't just lit. It was alive. Neon tubes burned with a strange intensity, crackling at the edges like they might explode. The letters flickered in a rhythm that matched the jackhammer beat behind his eyes, an epileptic tattoo of light and shadow, light and shadow, light and shadow.

And above it all, mounted high on the building's crumbling facade, the grotesque crown jewel: a giant **neon bust of Abraham Lincoln**.

It wasn't dignified or noble. It was cartoonish and terrifying, cheeks too hollow, jaw too square, beard glowing like radioactive moss. The eyes were wide open, two pulsing white circles that glowed and dimmed with the rest of the sign. There was no expression, just the eternal stare of a dead man forced into advertising discount vodka.

Lincoln's glowing head loomed above the liquor store like some twisted American deity. A sentinel of sorrows. His face buzzed and pulsed, etched in fractured gas and glass, blinking down in that cold, judgmental strobe.

Every time the sign flashed to full brightness, the entire room lit up behind him, walls washed in a sick neon bath, shadows warping and crawling like insects. Then darkness again. Then blinding red. Then gone.

It felt choreographed. Like the light was breathing with him, or for him. Like he'd been plugged into it, a machine syncing its horror to his heartbeat.

Outside, the street was empty. No cars. No people. Just the blinking sign and the faint buzz of bad wiring, vibrating through the window frame and into his fingertips.

He didn't breathe for a long moment. Couldn't.

The light flared again, so bright this time it erased the street, the buildings, the world. Just red. A wall of it.

When it blinked out, Lincoln's face lingered for a split second behind his eyelids, burned into his retinas like an afterimage from hell.

He choked on his own breath.

"No," he whispered.

"No—no, no, no."

"This just isn't fucking possible."

He staggered back from the window like it had struck him. Like Lincoln himself had reached through the glass and shoved him. He crashed into the foot of the bed, caught himself, then slammed his fist down hard on the mattress, again and again, until his arm throbbed.

He was shaking. Breathing like a wounded animal.

"You motherfucker," he growled. "You *planned* this, didn't you?"

He stood, pacing now, arms flailing, legs weak, spitting rage like venom into the buzzing air. "You just couldn't leave me alone. Not after the girl. Not after the job. The house. The fucking car. No—now you've got me crawling across the goddamn country, and what do I see the second I open my eyes? *You.* AGAIN."

He lunged toward the window, pressed both palms to the glass like he might shove the entire world away.

"I get it! Message received! You win! You smug, dead-eyed bastard!"

He slammed a hand against the glass. The neon light flared again, lighting up the room in red and horror. His shadow stretched long and warped behind him.

"Is this vengeance, huh? Did I insult you in some past life? Were you there in the void, sharpening your wrath for *me*?"

He turned, grabbing the lamp off the nightstand and hurling it across the room. It exploded against the wall, showering the floor with sparks and cheap ceramic shards.

"You weren't content with being on the penny, the five, Mount Rushmore—oh no, not enough! Now you've gotta pop up like a goddamn ghost every time I blink too slow!"

He clutched his temples, knees buckling, teeth grinding. The neon pulsed again, red, gone, red, gone. Like a heartbeat synced to madness.

"What *are* you?" he barked. "Some cosmic debt collector? A presidential poltergeist? You've got your own liquor store now—is that it? You trying to finish me off with rotgut and shame?"

He stumbled, fell hard onto the bed, then dragged himself up again like he couldn't stand to stay down in front of that light.

"This is personal," he hissed. "Don't pretend it's not. You could've haunted anyone. You picked me. Why?"

There was no answer. Only the glow. The hum. The endless, pulsing judgment from across the street.

He reached for the curtain, ready to rip it down, but froze, because that would mean not seeing it. And *not seeing it* might be worse.

So instead, he sank slowly to the floor, head thudding softly against the wall, knees drawn up, arms slack at his sides. The neon glow strobed across his face, red, black, red again, like some hellish heartbeat synced to his unraveling mind.

His chest hitched. Once. Twice.

Then came the sound, half-laugh, half-sob, scraped from the back of his throat like rusted metal grinding loose.

"Oh my God…" he whispered, the words torn and hollow. "You win. You *fucking win*."

His voice cracked into a strange, choked giggle, then back into something closer to weeping. "Is that what you wanted? Huh? You smug, horse-faced motherfucker?"

He was shaking now, caught between hysteria and collapse. The kind of unhinged fury that came not from fear, but from *exhaustion*.

"What more do you want from me?" he shouted suddenly, jerking forward like the question had burst out of his ribs. "The girl's gone. The job's gone. The house. The fucking Range Rover. You reached into every corner of my life and hollowed it out. What's left?"

He was laughing harder now, tears streaking down his cheeks, wild eyes fixed on that monstrous neon head across the street.

"Is this the part where I confess? Beg? Offer my soul up like a goddamn Lincoln penny in some cosmic vending machine? What can I *do*, huh? What will finally end this?"

He pressed both fists against his temples, rocking slightly, like if he could just squeeze hard enough, he might force the madness out.

"I *give up*, you rotten son of a bitch," he snarled. "You win. Take the rest. Take it all. Just—just stop. *Please*."

But Lincoln said nothing.

He just glowed, silent, unwavering, electric.

A slow, pulsing red light that seemed less like illumination and more like a heartbeat, an unblinking, judgmental pulse that seeped into the walls, into the air, into his skin.

It was the glow of something ancient and relentless, a cold, spectral sentinel that watched him with unyielding, wordless verdicts, an electric pulse of accusation and condemnation that thrummed with quiet menace, never fading, never forgiving.

A bright red interrogation lamp in a cosmic third degree from the grave, beaming across time, across reason.

As his eyelids grew heavy and the weight of fatigue dragged him down, the relentless flashing began to shift—a slow metamorphosis from harsh electric glare into a twisted lullaby. Not one of comfort, but of malice, whispered in hues of blood-red and shadow-black. The pulse became a cruel rhythm, hypnotic and cold, a visual chant of torment woven from the dark corners of his mind.

This was no innocent melody. It was a sinister song, sung by the very nemesis that haunted him, an unyielding phantom lurking beyond the veil, threading its venom into every flicker of light. The glow no longer illuminated the room; it devoured it, wrapping him in a velvet shroud of electric menace.

With each slow pulse, the lullaby dragged him closer to oblivion, a final surrender to the endless watching, the unceasing judgment. The red light throbbed like a heartbeat, steady and unrelenting, as he slipped, fading, drifting, into the dark abyss of sleep.

Chapter 21: Wire Transfer

The relentless neon Lincoln head outside the motel window was still glowing, still pulsing, its red halo now clashing with the soft creep of morning light. As if it refused to concede to the sun. As if the sign itself was in open defiance of dawn.

Michael sat hunched on the edge of the bed, elbows on his knees, staring at his wallet.

He rubbed his eyes, gritty with dried sweat and bad dreams. His mouth tasted like stale booze, and the back of his neck was slick with a cold sheen. His clothes still smelled like the bar. Cheap perfume and cheaper beer.

Then, reluctantly, he reached for the phone.

It rang once. Twice.

"Michael?" came Joseph's voice, tired but alert.

Michael cleared his throat. "Yeah. It's me."

"You alright?"

A pause.

"No. Not really."

Another pause.

"What happened?"

Michael pressed his palm to his forehead. "I got… I got taken for a ride. Literally. Some girl. Some bar. I don't even know. It's all a blur."

Joseph said nothing at first. Just the sound of breathing through the line.

"She drugged me, I think. Cleaned me out. Wallet was still here—just empty."

"Jesus."

"Yeah."

Joseph's voice was calm, measured. "You still in Cheyenne?"

"Yeah."

"Okay. You need help?"

Michael nodded again, then remembered. "Yeah. I can't stay here though. I've got to get the hell out of this town. There's a bank in Rock Springs. If you can wire some money there, I'll pick it up and move on."

"I've got a little cash stashed in the glovebox," Michael added quickly. "Not much, but enough for a cheap motel tonight."

"I just won't have enough to finish the trip. I'll just need enough to get the rest of the way there."

"You've still got your ID?"

"Yeah."

"Alright," Joseph said. "Bank only. I'll send it through Western Union or direct-to-branch. You'll get a transaction number."

Michael nodded again. "Thanks."

"You sound like hell, Mike."

"I feel worse."

Silence for a beat. Then Joseph asked quietly, "You sure you're okay to drive?"

"I have to be. I can't sit here with that goddamn Lincoln sign flashing at me."

Joseph didn't laugh. "Alright. I'll send the details soon."

Michael stood, stiff and slow, as if gravity had increased overnight.

"Thanks, Joe."

"You'll be alright. Just keep moving."

Michael hung up. The red glow was still there, smeared against the inside of his eyelids even with his eyes closed. He grabbed his bag, what little of it remained, and stepped into the daylight. The motel door slammed behind him like a vault locking.

No rearview mirror glances.

No need.

He was done with Cheyenne.

Chapter 22: No More Cheyenne

The headache settled in like an unwanted passenger, wedged behind his eyes, pulsing in rhythm with every bump in the road. Michael gripped the steering wheel tighter than he needed to, his knuckles white, the Pinto wagon rattling beneath him as if it too wanted out of Cheyenne.

He didn't look back.

The neon Lincoln head still burned in his mind, its red glow seared behind his eyelids. Even now, in daylight, it haunted him like a retinal ghost. The sun was up, but it felt pale and weak—no match for what had burned through the night.

The drive to Rock Springs wasn't far, just under four hours, but he planned to make it feel like a whole day. He didn't turn on the radio. No music, no news, no noise. Just the wind screaming through the cracked window and the occasional cough from the engine.

He passed signs without reading them. Stared through the windshield like it was a tunnel. Each mile stretched longer than it should've. He wasn't in a hurry to arrive, he just wanted to *not be* in Cheyenne anymore.

His head throbbed. The nausea came in slow waves, curling up from his gut and retreating again. He knew it was from whatever they'd slipped into his drink. He'd tried to shake it off, but it clung to him, like the shame.

The Pinto swayed in the wind as trucks passed him on the interstate. He didn't care. He barely noticed. The emptiness around him suited him, vast plains and scrubland, nothing to reflect back at him. No neon. No names.

Chapter 23: Sentinel at 8,640 Feet

The highway stretched out ahead, a scorched ribbon cut through the vast, arid land. The heat rising off the asphalt blurred the edges of the world, bending the horizon into a shimmering mirage that teased tired eyes. Dust clung to the faded yellow lines like a memory refusing to fade away.

Inside the car, the stale scent of recycled air mixed with faint hints of old leather and the ghost of coffee long spilled. His hands rested on the steering wheel, white-knuckled but steady, fingers drumming out a rhythm lost somewhere between impatience and exhaustion.

Outside, the sun was a harsh overseer, relentless and unyielding. Sweat gathered along the back of his neck, slipping beneath the collar of his shirt like a cold thread. He didn't bother wiping it away, not yet.

The radio crackled to life, a thin band of static curling through the speakers. He twisted the dial, hunting for something that didn't sound like ghosts whispering through the ether. Stations came and went like fleeting shadows, a burst of country twang, a snippet of a preacher's sermon, the faint strains of a pop song half-swallowed by interference.

Then a voice cut through the noise. Sharp. Angry.

"*You who listen in darkness, who walk the crooked path of sin, hear me now!*" The preacher's voice was harsh, relentless, a firebrand cast into the desert heat. "*Turn*

163

from your wicked ways or face the eternal flames that await the unrepentant!"

The words struck him like a slap, reverberating in the cramped space of the car. His grip tightened on the wheel, pulse quickening. He could almost feel the preacher's gaze piercing through the radio waves, judging him in the silence between breaths.

For a long moment, he let the sermon fill the car, let the fire and brimstone wash over his nerves, setting them alight with a strange, uncomfortable energy.

Then, with a snap, he turned the dial.

A country song tried to claim the silence next, a slow, twangy lament about broken hearts and desert storms. The voice cracked, the guitar strings jangling like they were straining under the weight of too many lost promises. The singer's voice was raw, almost pleading.

He sneered.

"Aw, fuck it," he muttered, and twisted the volume knob all the way down, letting the silence fall like a curtain.

No music. No sermons. Just the hum of the engine and the steady pulse of the tires on the road.

Outside the window, the landscape sprawled wide and empty, a lunar canvas of cracked earth and twisted sagebrush. The air smelled dry and ancient, carrying the faintest hint of creosote and dust stirred up by the passing breeze.

The sky was a pale dome of blue, stretched impossibly high and unbroken. A few wispy clouds drifted like forgotten thoughts.

He blinked slowly, letting his gaze wander over the barren beauty. The emptiness seemed to breathe with him, a vast, patient presence that demanded nothing and offered no judgment.

The weight pressing down on his chest loosened a little, the tight knot of tension unwinding just enough to let him breathe deeper.

His breath came in slow, deliberate draws. The rise and fall of his chest a fragile rhythm, steadying his restless mind.

He glanced down at his hands, noticing how his fingers had relaxed, the knuckles softening.

For a moment, the road was no longer a pathway away from something, but simply a stretch of blacktop beneath an endless sky.

He let himself imagine that maybe, just maybe, he was moving toward something, too.

The tires hummed steadily beneath him, a lullaby of rubber on asphalt. He reached for the air conditioning, flipping the switch, and a thin stream of cool air swept over his face, carrying a fleeting relief from the relentless heat.

The road curled ahead in gentle arcs, inviting but unmarked. No signs, no markers, no hints of destination. Just miles and miles of open space.

He leaned back slightly in the seat, letting the car settle into its rhythm. The fatigue weighed heavy in his eyelids, but he fought it, forcing his gaze forward.

The radio remained silent.

Outside, the world was a blur of ochre and burnt sienna, the hills rolling like slow waves frozen in time. The occasional silhouette of a dead tree stood stark against the horizon, a dark fingerprint on the pale earth.

Somewhere far off, a hawk cried out, its sharp call breaking the stillness for a brief moment before sinking back into silence.

He thought about how small he was, how fragile, a speck swallowed by the vastness outside his window.

The loneliness wasn't new. It was old, worn, like the seat cushions beneath him.

He welcomed it, though, this hollow quiet that swallowed the noise of life.

No demands. No expectations. Just the road and the sky and the endless hum of the engine.

Minutes passed, or maybe hours. Time seemed to stretch and warp, measured only by the slow dance of shadows across the dashboard.

He reached down, pulling a bottle of water from the cup holder, took a long drink. The cool liquid slid down his throat, soothing the dryness.

He wiped his mouth with the back of his hand and looked out again.

The sun had climbed higher, its glare intensifying. Sweat traced thin rivers down his temples.

Still, he drove on.

The air inside the car was thick with exhaustion and caffeine—the restless buzz from too many energy drinks tangling with the deep-rooted weariness that pressed heavy on his bones. His eyelids flickered, stubbornly refusing to close, even as his mind pushed through the fog, sharp and jittery beneath the surface.

The road ahead stretched empty and endless, a ribbon of black carving through rolling brown hills that looked like forgotten waves frozen in time. The dry earth cracked in the heat, dust stirred faintly in the faint breeze, lifting in lazy swirls that caught the afternoon sun.

Nothing for miles. No cars. No signs of life beyond the occasional scrubby brush.

The silence outside was dense, a vast quiet that seemed to press against the thin glass of the windshield.

He swallowed hard, feeling the dryness in his throat that no sip of water could quite wash away. The grip on the steering wheel tightened, knuckles whitening, fingers tapping an erratic beat as the hum of the engine filled the space.

His gaze flicked from the road to the hills, then back again, eyes aching but refusing to rest.

In the corner of his vision, the dashboard clock glowed softly, a dull reminder that time was still moving, though it felt like the world around him had paused.

A sudden yawn caught him by surprise, sharp and dry, like a crack in the dam. He clenched his jaw and rubbed at his eyes, blinking rapidly to stave off the pull of sleep.

Ahead, a faint sign emerged against the dusty brown, weathered and peeling, half-hidden by the haze.

Rest Area – Next Right.

His heart jumped a fraction, a brief flare of relief mingling with the persistent tightness that had been sitting in his chest for days.

He flicked on his turn signal and eased the wheel, following the off-ramp that curved into a shallow valley between the hills.

The road narrowed here, gravel crunching beneath the tires as the car slowed to a crawl.

He felt the tension in his muscles loosen slightly, the relentless forward motion easing into something more manageable.

The rest area appeared like an island of civilization amid the barren sweep—simple, utilitarian, its cracked concrete and faded paint blending into the earth around it.

A few cars sat scattered, coated in dust and the dull sheen of neglect.

He pulled into an empty spot, the engine ticking as it cooled.

Stepping out, the heat hit him immediately, a dry wall of air carrying the scent of sun-baked earth and distant sage.

He stretched his arms above his head, the stiffness in his back cracking with relief.

Around him, the hills rolled gently, their muted browns and tans shifting under the bright sky.

The only sound was the soft whistle of wind weaving through the sparse brush.

He took a slow, deliberate breath, filling his lungs with the dry air, tasting grit on his tongue.

For the first time in hours, the noise inside his head quieted just a fraction.

His eyes drifted to the horizon, where the land stretched on, empty and infinite.

The sun hung heavy, casting long shadows that stretched like fingers across the ground.

He let himself sink into the moment, the vastness, the silence, the strange, flickering calm.

For now, the world felt still.

The door creaked softly as he pushed it open, stepping into the rest area building with the hollow echo of his boots against cracked linoleum. The air inside was stale, tinged with the faint chemical bite of industrial cleaner and something faintly sour—leftover traces of a hundred travelers passing through.

Fluorescent lights flickered overhead, casting a pale, sickly glow that made the peeling paint on the walls seem even more tired. The scent of damp tile and worn plastic hung thick, mingling with the faint buzz of an old, sputtering fan stuck in the corner.

Rows of metal stalls lined the narrow room, their chipped doors hanging slightly ajar or stubbornly shut, some bearing graffiti, scrawled names, crude jokes, faded declarations of love or rebellion. The faint drip of a leaky faucet echoed somewhere down the hall.

He moved with slow, deliberate steps, the scrape of his shoes against the floor mingling with the distant hum of a flickering overhead light. The mirror above the cracked sink reflected a man he barely recognized, lines etched deeper, eyes shadowed, skin pale and drawn.

He washed his hands, the cold water running over skin rough and dry. The basin was chipped at the edges, stained by time and neglect. He glanced up, catching his tired reflection once more before turning toward the exit.

Stepping out the back door, the sudden rush of outside air hit him, a dry, warm breath carrying the scent of sun-baked earth and dust stirred by a light wind.

He hesitated, momentarily disoriented by the brightness after the dimness inside.

Looking around, his eyes caught the wide-open expanse behind the building, a patch of gravel and sparse scrub, rolling brown hills melting into the distance under a relentless sun.

Then, his gaze drifted upward.

And there it was.

A massive, grotesque head looming above the rest area like a dark sentinel, its features exaggerated and worn, the bronze mottled by years of sun and wind. The eyes seemed to bore down on him, cold and judgmental, frozen in an eternal stare that made the hair on his neck rise.

He stumbled back involuntarily, heart pounding, breath catching in his throat.

The statue's presence was absurd, out of place, a hulking, silent judge in the middle of nowhere.

For a moment, everything else, the quiet hills, the cracked concrete, the weary hours on the road, faded away, swallowed by the oppressive weight of that terrible, staring face.

The face was Lincoln, sort of, but stretched and twisted like a carnival mirror reflection gone wrong. His forehead was a cracked wasteland of deep wrinkles, carved so sharply they looked like the scars of a lifetime's worth of silent screams and hard, bitter regrets.

The brows weren't just furrowed; they were heaving ridges of metal, heavy and uneven, as if the weight of every broken promise in American history had crushed down onto that forehead and left it trembling in perpetual disapproval.

His eyes—oh god, the eyes—were cavernous pits of dull bronze shadow, sunken far too deep beneath a brow that threatened to fall over them like storm clouds. They stared out with a predatory stillness, like a beast waiting patiently to pounce on every secret, every failure, every whispered sin.

The nose was oddly elongated, sharp-edged and unsettling, too narrow and too long, like some grotesque caricature painted by a mad artist. It jutted out above a pair of thin, tightly pursed lips that seemed to sneer even in stone, an eternal smirk of contempt that promised he knew everything, and he was unimpressed.

The cheeks were hollowed, almost skeletal, with veins and folds etched deep into the bronze like ancient riverbeds drying up under a merciless sun. Wrinkles cascaded down in harsh, jagged lines that suggested not just age but a lifetime spent gnashing teeth in silent fury.

The jaw was square and clenched like a fist, frozen in a permanent expression of judgment, the kind that felt like a slap before a sentence was even delivered.

A strange, almost imperceptible curl tugged at one corner of the mouth, hinting at some private, bitter joke, maybe at Mary Todd's expense, or some long-forgotten cabinet meeting gone terribly wrong.

The neck was thick and corded, veins bulging like ropes tied tight around a prisoner's throat, the whole head perched awkwardly on a rough slab of granite that looked like it had been ripped straight from the earth.

Around the base, small rivulets of rust bled down like tears, bronze tears, mournful and mocking all at once.

The wind whipped around the statue, tugging at his coat, carrying faint whispers of accusation and regret, as if the bronze head was speaking in tongues only the guilty could hear.

He felt it, this monstrous sentinel wasn't just watching. It was waiting. Judging. Calculating. Ready to call out everything he thought he'd left behind on the road.

For a moment, the world tilted. The sun-baked hills, the cracked concrete, even the remainder of the rest area faded into a backdrop for this towering oracle of doom.

And above it all, that face loomed, an ancient, merciless reminder that some judgments never fade.

His feet froze. Not from fear, not quite, but from that deep, involuntary jolt the brain makes when it can't decide if it's dreaming or being hunted.

For several seconds, he just stared, mouth slightly open, head tilted like a confused dog trying to decode a war crime. There were no signs. No warning. No reason. Just this. A looming, hideous bronze head of Abraham goddamn Lincoln squatting in the hills like some presidential Sphinx watching over the highway with eternal disdain.

"...What the fuck," he muttered. It came out slow and flat, as if the words were afraid to disturb whatever dark ritual was happening here.

He took a step back. Then another. His sneakers crunched in the gravel as he turned in a small circle, half-expecting to see cameras, or hidden speakers, or maybe a Ranger Rick popping out from behind a bush to say, "Ha! Gotcha! It's Lincoln Day!"

But no one came.

It was just him. And that face.

Lincoln's grimace seemed to deepen in the shifting light. The bronze shadows cast under his hollow eyes made it look like he hadn't slept since Gettysburg. That thousand-yard stare wasn't just long, it was personal. It reached into the marrow. It said, you know what you did.

He tried to laugh. A short, brittle bark of air that bounced off the hills and died with a whimper.

"Who the hell... puts this here?" he said aloud, as if speaking might draw someone else into the absurdity. "At a rest stop? Like—right after the urinals?"

No answer.

The wind picked up, brushing the collar of his jacket, carrying that dry, restless whisper again. Not words exactly, but a feeling, like something had been watching him for a while now and finally decided to show itself.

His eyes darted to the empty hills. To the building behind him. To the highway beyond, quiet and glinting in the sun. Everything still. Everything silent. But the feeling persisted.

He turned back to the statue.

The wrinkles in that face seemed deeper now. Or maybe they'd always been like that and his brain was just catching up. It wasn't the stoic Lincoln from textbooks or coins. This wasn't a symbol. This was a warning.

It looked like Lincoln had seen things, seen him.

Not just the surface stuff, either. Not the forgotten parking tickets or bad breakups. No, this Lincoln had

174

dug deeper. Into the stuff he didn't say aloud. The thoughts he didn't write down. The weak, hungry parts he tried to bury under noise and caffeine and motion.

And now Honest Abe was here. A ten-foot conscience in bronze.

He squinted up at the giant face, one hand shielding his eyes from the glare. "I didn't ask for this, man," he said, trying to laugh again. "I just had to take a piss."

Still nothing.

The silence became oppressive. Like air being slowly sucked out of the sky.

Something in his chest tightened.

His hands curled into fists without him noticing. He could feel his jaw tensing, could feel the heat rising up the back of his neck. This wasn't funny anymore. It wasn't quirky. It wasn't some weird roadside Americana kitsch. It was too much. Too targeted.

He took a step closer to the statue, like it might blink or flinch.

"You judging me, huh?" he said, louder now. "You got something to say? Go ahead. Fucking say it."

Bronze Lincoln, of course, said nothing. He just stared. All-seeing. All-knowing. All-judging. Monumentally smug.

"Are you fucking serious?" he said, louder now, voice sharp and rising in pitch. "No. No. Nope. Not again. This—this is bullshit."

He threw his hands in the air and laughed, a jagged, breathless bark that had no humor in it. It came

175

from somewhere between his chest and his teeth, like a noise that had been trying to get out for days.

Because it figured. Of course it did. Of course it was Lincoln. Again.

He stared up at that enormous bronze skull, that stern immortal face like a pissed-off demigod carved by someone who hated comfort and smiles.

"You've got to be kidding me," he said, eyes wide, pacing now in small, agitated loops in front of the statue. "You're here? In the middle of goddamn nowhere? After all the shit this week, this month, and I stop to take a piss and you show up? Again?"

His voice cracked on the last word. The desert wind licked at his back. The statue didn't blink. Didn't move.

"Fuck you, Abe. Do I owe you something? Is there some kind of cosmic punishment for not kissing your ass and paying proper homage to you?"

He stepped closer, jabbing a finger toward the base of the granite. "You think I don't see it? You've been there. At the edge of every fucking thing. It's clear as day now."

His throat was raw now, and his eyes burned, not with tears, but with that dry, electric sting of someone just on the edge of unraveling. Too many hours on the road. Too many gas station coffees. Too much silence. And too much of that face.

"You're the High Plains Sentinel of Shame," he hissed. "Watching over an interstate urinal stop at 8,640 feet. What did I do to earn this? What—did I use the Gettysburg Address as a drink coaster in a past life?"

The wind howled in reply.

Lincoln said nothing. As always.

That made it worse.

He rubbed his eyes hard, like he might wipe away the last five minutes.

Then he turned on his heel and walked fast, too fast, toward his car. He didn't run. He wasn't giving Lincoln that satisfaction. But he didn't look back, either. Because somehow, in some cracked-out corner of his overstimulated brain, he was absolutely sure that if he did...

Lincoln would be smiling.

"Sentinel of Shame," he muttered again, the words sour in his mouth. "Eight thousand goddamn feet of judgment... all for taking a piss."

He paused, chest heaving.

Then something in him snapped completely.

"You know what? Fuck you," he shouted, voice echoing off the hills and scrub brush. "You're stuck here. Stuck, in this forsaken shithole, watching over the toilets, you miserable motherfucker!"

His finger jabbed wildly in the air, accusatory, almost trembling.

"I'm out there, driving. Moving. You get that? I'm free! I can leave! I can go wherever the hell I want, and you—"

He stomped toward the granite base, boots crunching gravel. "—you just sit here. Watching old people take dumps and truckers jerk off in stall number three. That's your afterlife? That's your grand legacy? Fuckin' roadside crypt keeper of broken bladders?"

He circled the statue now, voice climbing, veins bulging in his neck. "Look at you. Look at that face. Judging me with your sunken little dead eyes and your twisted hollow face. You're not noble. You're not wise."

The wind answered again, dry and distant, but he was past hearing it. Words poured out of him like pressure from a blown gasket.

"What, you got nothing to say now? You've got a million speeches in granite and bronze, but not a damn word for me? You stare like you've got it all figured out, like I'm some lost cause crawling through your field of honor and sacrifice—but you don't know me. You don't know shit about me."

"You look down on me… judging." His voice lowered. "I'm not ashamed. You should be ashamed."

He leaned in close now, nose almost brushing the oxidized edge of the slab.

"Sideways looks won't work on me, cocksucker."

He took another step closer, stared up at that bronze skull, and said—quietly, venomously—

"You want a tip, Abe, you ugly fuck? Don't go to the movies tonight."

A beat of silence. No echo. Just wind.

Then, almost to himself, the words came again—softer, darker:

"Spoiler alert… you might not like the ending."

The words just hung there. Hot. Sharp. Wrong.

Even the wind seemed to step back.

His hands were shaking. Sweat traced a cold path down his spine.

Somewhere deep inside, a voice whispered: You're yelling at a statue.

But another voice answered, louder: "Fuck him."

He stood there panting, face flushed, eyes wide and wild, breath fogging in the dry air. A bead of sweat rolled down his temple.

And then, footsteps.

Soft. Shuffling. Approaching from the side path by the building.

He turned just in time to see an elderly woman, mid-seventies maybe, wide-brimmed sunhat, sensible shoes, purse clutched tightly to her chest, freeze mid-step.

They locked eyes.

She stared at him. He stared at her. The silence screamed.

Her gaze shifted slowly to the statue, then back to him, taking in his wild posture, the sweat, the clenched fists, the thousand-yard crazy in his eyes. Her expression hardened into a kind of polite horror, as though she'd just caught him pants-down screaming at a tombstone.

"Morning," she said stiffly, voice tight, brittle.

He nodded, muttering, "Yeah. Yep. Just... stretching."

She gave a nervous half-smile and quickened her pace toward the restroom entrance, giving the statue—and him—a wide berth.

He stood frozen for a second, then rubbed his face hard with both hands.

"Jesus Christ," he muttered under his breath. "Get it together. You're yelling at Lincoln in public now. Good job, man."

He turned and began walking fast, half-stumble, half-retreat, across the cracked pavement toward his car.

"Stretching," he repeated under his breath with a bitter laugh. "Great save. Nailed it. Totally normal guy. Nothing to see here, ma'am. Just out here threatening dead presidents like a totally balanced adult."

He yanked the driver's side door open, dropped into the seat like a getaway driver in his own nervous breakdown.

The silence inside the car was thick and absolute.

He stared straight ahead, hands still on the wheel.

Don't look back.

He looked back.

Lincoln was still there.

Unmoving.

Disgusted.

"Fuck," he whispered, turning the key in the ignition.

Chapter 24: Rock Springs

The Pinto wagon shuddered back onto the highway, gravel spitting from the tires as Michael floored it out of the rest stop like it had personally offended him.

His hands were still trembling. Not from fear, but from rage, disbelief, exhaustion, some unnamable combination that settled under his skin like static. The Sentinel still loomed in his mind, that grotesque Lincoln head with its dead bronze eyes, watching, judging. His rant still echoed in the silence of the car.

"What the fuck was that?"

He said it out loud. Again. Like a challenge to no one.

No answer came, just the low drone of the engine, the hum of tires over cracked asphalt, the broken wiper arm rattling against the windshield with every gust of crosswind.

The sky ahead was wide open, gray-blue with streaks of ochre where the clouds broke. There was no color in him. He felt scraped raw, like he'd been hollowed out at the rest stop and was now just muscle memory behind the wheel.

He didn't care about speed limits. The Pinto had its own limitations anyway. The steering wheel drifted left without warning. He corrected it absently with one hand while the other hung loose out the open window.

At one point, he laughed. Just one dry, bitter bark.

That fucking statue.

The miles passed, scrubby hills rising and falling around him. There was no music. No thoughts that could form. Just flashes: Lincoln. Kayla. The empty wallet. The note on the counter. The potted plant exploding against drywall.

A flashing road sign broke the loop:

ROCK SPRINGS — 47 MILES

He didn't exhale until he saw it.

Not because Rock Springs meant anything.

But because it wasn't *here*.

He took the first exit that looked halfway commercial. A tired-looking strip of buildings crouched low against the wind, gas station, pawn shop, liquor store.

Michael turned into the lot of a squat, windowless building with a crooked sign that read: LUCKY MOUNTAIN LIQUOR & NOODLE HOUSE.

The parking lot was cracked concrete with tufts of grass growing through. But what caught his eye was the Buddha — big, round-bellied, and cast in what looked like stone, squatting right near the front of the building. Its smile was soft. Eyes closed. Like it knew something he didn't.

Michael parked in the spot closest to it. The Pinto wheezed as he shut off the engine.

He stepped out, cracked neck and back, and took a longer look.

For a moment, he just stood there, staring at the statue, arms limp at his sides.

It didn't leer. It didn't glow. It didn't accuse.

It just sat.

Peaceful. Still.

He nodded to it, actually nodded, like it was a person, and walked inside.

The store was fluorescent-lit and smelled like old fryer grease. There was a dusty red menu board above a worn countertop to the left, the "Chinese" part of the operation. A lone flat-screen TV bolted to the corner wall flickered with local news. The volume was low.

He grabbed a six-pack of whatever was cold and cheap. Something pale. Forgettable. Also ordered some sesame chicken and white rice without even thinking.

The woman behind the counter bagged it all without small talk.

As she counted change, a loud commercial blasted from the TV overhead.

"Tonight's Powerball is up to $118 million! Someone in Wyoming could be the lucky winner..."

Michael looked up at the screen. Cartoon graphics of dollar signs and bouncing balls danced around.

He fished in his pocket, pulled out a crumpled five, and slid it across the counter. "One ticket," he said.

She printed it, handed it over without expression.

He folded it in half and tucked it into his shirt pocket.

As he stepped back outside, the Buddha was still there, still smiling, still at peace.

Michael gave a faint, crooked smile.

"Better than Lincoln," he muttered.

Then he got in the car and headed to find a motel.

The first squat row of motels came into view like a mirage stitched along the edge of the highway, flat-roofed, sun-faded, and half-swallowed by decades of blowing dust. Michael took the next exit without signaling, the Pinto wheezing its protest as he guided it down the off-ramp. A weather-warped sign creaked in the wind: **Sweet Dreams Motel** — two of the plastic letters missing, the "M" dangling by a screw.

He pulled into the gravel lot, tires crunching slow over broken glass and bottle caps. The **lot was large and mostly empty**, stretching wide in all directions like nobody wanted to stay too long. The building was a single-story strip of identical doors, each numbered in crooked brass digits. A few were occupied, trucks backed in, tarps flapping in beds, windows curtained with towels from the inside. One guy in a mesh tank top smoked on a plastic chair and didn't look up. Another room had its TV flickering blue against the window, even in daylight.

Michael parked near the end. As the Pinto sputtered to a stop, the engine gave one final cough and a dry metallic wheeze, like it had been holding its breath the whole time.

He stayed in the car a minute.

The silence felt thick.

The headache had dulled to a background hum now. The town seemed still, too still. There was no wind, not even birdsong. Just the dull electric hum of vacancy.

Eventually, he stepped out.

The sun hit harder out here, reflecting off the bleached concrete. He blinked behind dry eyes and made his way toward the office, a glass cube off to the side of the lot, advertising "Low Weekly Rates" in sun-warped vinyl.

The door chimed as he entered.

Inside, it smelled like dust and lemon cleaner. A small fan oscillated behind the counter but didn't seem to cool anything. The clerk didn't stand, a woman maybe in her sixties, silver hair in a loose ponytail, face half-shadowed under a wall-mounted television. She didn't smile.

"One night," Michael said, reaching into his back pocket. "Cash."

She glanced up, her eyes taking the measure of him in one practiced sweep.

"That'll be forty-two even," she said, voice dry as the Wyoming wind.

He handed over three crumpled twenties.

She gave him a metal key on a green plastic tag. Room 9.

"Park on the far end of the lot. Don't block the ice machine."

Michael nodded and left without another word.

Room 9 was at the far end of the strip, two doors down from the ice machine and just past a row of flickering porch lights that hadn't been changed since the Bush administration.

Michael parked and killed the engine, and sat there a moment, letting the last vibrations of the Pinto settle into silence. The gravel lot was wide and mostly empty, with only a few other vehicles scattered about, old trucks, rusted sedans, a motorcycle draped in a sun-bleached tarp. A silence hung over the place that wasn't peaceful, just vacant.

He stepped out. The motel's outer wall was a faded stucco the color of old mustard. The walkway was cracked concrete, cigarette burns dotting the surface like scars. Room 9's door was a peeling beige slab with a greasy handle and a worn welcome mat that read *"Live, Laugh, Leave"* in half-faded letters.

He unlocked it with a jangle of the green plastic tag and pushed it open.

The room smelled faintly of mildew and stale air, a mix of freon, synthetic linen spray, and years of human exhaustion. The A/C unit beneath the window groaned to life automatically, spitting out a puff of lukewarm air before settling into a high, whining hum.

Inside, the room was a study in minimalism by neglect.

A single bed sat low to the floor, its thin mattress bowed in the middle like it had grown tired of trying. The coverlet was a scratchy burgundy, patterned with abstract swirls that looked like faded blood splatter under the wrong lighting. Two lumpy pillows leaned against the headboard, one visibly flatter than the other, both stained at the edges.

A nightstand stood beside the bed, its faux wood laminate chipped at the corners. On it, a yellowed notepad advertising a long-defunct pizza place, and a remote wrapped in a greasy plastic sleeve that crinkled when touched. The lamp had no shade, just a naked bulb that cast a sickly halo over the wall.

Opposite the bed, an old, worn dresser supported an old tube television with dials instead of buttons. The screen was dark, but the power light blinked red as if trying to stay awake. Above it hung a crooked painting, some abstract desert scene that tried too hard to look peaceful.

The bathroom door was open. Inside: green tile, a rust-stained sink, and a toilet that groaned once when flushed like it wanted you to apologize for the trouble.

Michael stood in the center of the room, the door clicking shut behind him.

No minibar. No coffee maker. Not even a phone.

But it had four walls. A door that locked. And for the moment, no neon Lincoln.

He dropped the small plastic bag onto the dresser, inside, his beer, the half pint of whiskey, and a white paper box of Chinese food beginning to sweat through. He removed the lottery ticket from his pocket and placed it into his wallet. "Who knows," he said.

Chapter 25: The Bank

Morning light filtered through a layer of dust on the windshield as the Pinto wagon pulled into the bank lot.

The bank stood squat and dull at the end of a half-empty strip mall, flat-roofed, beige brick, windows sun-bleached and tinted blue. Above the door, a plastic sign read: **First Western Credit Union**, some of the letters yellowing at the edges. A faded American flag hung limply from a metal pole near the entrance, fluttering weakly in the wind.

Michael pulled into a parking spot two spaces from the door, engine rattling into silence. The lot was quiet, a few minivans, a landscaping truck with a sagging trailer, and a rusted Ford Taurus sunbathing in the corner. It didn't feel dangerous. It felt like Tuesday.

He sat for a moment, eyes closed, breathing in slow. His headache had faded but not gone. There was a light fuzz around the edges of his thoughts — not quite pain, just pressure, like his skull was wearing an old wool cap that didn't fit.

He reached into the passenger seat, grabbed the wrinkled withdrawal instructions Joseph had texted him, and folded them into his jacket pocket. Then he grabbed his wallet, checked again: lottery ticket, ID, that last $10 bill. He wasn't broke, not yet, but this was about survival. The wired money was the last thread.

He stepped out, letting the door shut itself behind him with a dull thud. The sun was high, but the air had bite. Clean, dry mountain air that made everything look sharper.

Michael pushed open the glass door. It gave a little resistance, as if reluctant to let him in.

A small bell chimed overhead, mechanical, shrill, and unnecessary in the sterile quiet of the lobby. The air inside was cooler than outside, overly conditioned and faintly metallic, like recycled breath and cleaning solution.

To the left, a row of fake plants stood frozen in ceramic pots. Ahead, four teller windows with faded red stanchions leading to a plexiglass sign that read: **PLEASE WAIT TO BE CALLED** in cheery blue font. Only two windows were open.

There were a few people ahead of him, a man in a reflective road-crew vest depositing a stack of checks, a middle-aged woman arguing quietly about overdraft fees, and an elderly couple trying to decipher their statement printouts.

The teller behind the glass barely looked up between transactions. She had a blonde ponytail that didn't move and long lavender nails that tapped quickly on the keyboard. The second teller, a young man with nervous eyes and a dress shirt one size too large, kept glancing toward the back hallway as if hoping to be rescued from the job.

A security guard sat on a stool near the door. Late sixties. Retired cop energy. Pale blue uniform stretched over a soft belly, baton holstered but looking mostly ceremonial. He wasn't armed—just a radio clipped to one shoulder and a badge that had seen better decades. He didn't make eye contact, just nodded slightly as Michael passed.

Near the middle of the lobby stood one of those tall, narrow desks, the kind meant for filling out deposit slips and loan envelopes. Michael walked to it and picked up a pen chained to the side.

He unfolded the note Joseph had sent, routing number, reference code, ID instructions, then looked down at the deposit/withdrawal slip already resting on the counter.

It was slightly crumpled, as if someone had picked it up and changed their mind.

No matter.

Michael began writing. Slowly. Carefully.

Michael finished writing out the numbers with stiff fingers, double-checked everything twice. Nothing seemed amiss. Just standard print. He stepped towards the next open window.

The woman with the lavender nails waved him over without looking up.

He slid the slip under the small gap at the bottom of the glass.

"Wire transfer," he said. "Should be under Joseph Torino."

She still didn't meet his eyes. Her fingers moved fast, typing. She glanced at the slip.

And then she paused.

She turned it over.

And froze.

Her posture stiffened. Her fingers left the keyboard. Her eyes scanned the back of the slip. Then flicked up — right at him, this time.

Not just looking.

Reading him.

Michael blinked, caught off guard.

"Something wrong?" he asked.

She didn't answer.

Instead, her hand disappeared below the counter, moving slowly, deliberately. Her other hand remained motionless beside the keyboard. The expression on her face had drained of all neutral professionalism — now it was careful. Controlled.

Michael shifted on his feet. "I just need the, what's going on?"

From the corner of the room, the old security guard stood. Slowly. Like a man remembering how to do it after too long.

He took one step forward.

Michael's heart stuttered.

"What's happening?"

Then the guard spoke, calm, casual, but with just enough tension behind it to make the hairs on Michael's arms stand up.

"Sir, I'm gonna need you to stay right where you are."

Michael frowned, baffled. "What? Why?"

The teller cleared her throat. "Sir, please don't make any sudden movements."

Her tone was firm now. Rehearsed.

That's when he saw it.

She still had the slip in her hand. And on the back, scrawled in thick black marker, probably from some bored teenager playing a prank earlier in the day:

THIS IS A HOLD-UP

Michael's eyes went wide.

"What the fuck—? No, no no no. That's not— I didn't write that!"

But the guard had already taken another step forward, one hand on the radio at his belt.

Michael's breath caught in his throat.

The room was shifting. Tilting. Flashing.

Just like the goddamn Lincoln sign.

Michael's legs moved before his brain could keep up.

"Hey!" the old security guard shouted, shuffling forward, one hand out, the other fumbling for the radio clipped to his chest.

Michael turned and ran.

The chain pen clattered against the stand-up desk as he passed it. The glass door burst open with a sharp jingle of bells, and he hit the sunlight like a prisoner escaping through a breach in the yard wall.

Gravel crunched under his feet as he sprinted to the Pinto.

His breath came ragged, too fast, too shallow.

Fumbling the keys.

Hands slick.

The door handle jammed for half a second, *of course* it did, but then gave, and he threw himself inside. The

193

Pinto groaned in protest as he twisted the key. Once. Twice—

Cough. Gasp.

Then the engine caught.

It didn't roar. It whimpered to life like an asthmatic bulldog.

He yanked the gearshift and floored it.

The tires spat a small tantrum of gravel before catching traction, and the Pinto fishtailed out of the lot, over a curb, and onto the road. He barely missed a landscaping trailer. Someone honked.

No sirens.

No one behind him.

He looked once in the rearview. The bank sat still. Peaceful. Undisturbed.

What the fuck just happened?

His heart was punching his ribs like it wanted out.

I didn't do anything, he told himself. *It was the slip. The goddamn slip.*

His thoughts spiraled.

She saw it. She thought it was me. But I didn't write it. I didn't even flip it over—

The steering wheel shook under his hands. He slowed down, trying to blend in. Trying not to look like a man who had just bolted from a bank like a lunatic.

He took a left. Then another. Random turns. Just to move.

His breathing slowed.

Still no sirens.

Still no flashing lights.

Maybe they won't come. Maybe they're checking cameras. Maybe it'll blow over.

But deep down, he knew.

He knew the second she hit that button.

He wasn't sure how long he drove, circling unfamiliar blocks, passing gas stations, faded strip malls, a shuttered bowling alley. But eventually—

He came back.

Pulled into the rear lot of the **Sweet Dreams Motel**.

Parked.

Turned off the ignition.

The Pinto ticked as it cooled, little mechanical pops breaking the stillness. Michael sat for just a second longer, watching dust swirl in the rearview like smoke from a fire he couldn't see. Then he moved.

Quick steps. Door slam. His feet crunched across the gravel as he made his way to his room. He unlocked the door fast, slipped inside.

The room was dim. The curtains were drawn. The beer still sat on the dresser, condensation now dried to sticky rings. The paper bag of Chinese food sagged in on itself.

He didn't touch any of it.

His heart was still thudding.

That slip... that fucking slip...

He ran both hands through his hair, pacing twice, then stopped short. His eyes darted to the duffel.

He started throwing things in with messy urgency, socks, a pair of jeans, deodorant, the half pint of whiskey. One flip-flop. Then the other.

He glanced to the window — still quiet outside.

Maybe I can make it out. Maybe they didn't follow. Maybe they're not coming.

He zipped the duffel, slung it over his shoulder.

Then—

Flash.

Red.

Blue.

Sirens.

He froze.

Outside, tires bit into the gravel. Radios crackled. Doors opened. Heavy boots hit the ground like a line of hammers.

They were here.

Not one car. Not two.

The lot was full.

Marked units. Unmarked. A black SUV with tinted windows. One cruiser angled in to block the exit. Another near the vending machines. The sun glinted off shotgun racks and side mirrors.

Michael's blood turned cold.

From behind the curtain, he watched a line of officers take position — some crouched behind vehicles, others holding radios to their shoulders. One had a shield. Another had a rifle.

"Come out with your hands up!"

A voice boomed through a megaphone. Sharp. Final.

Michael edged toward the window, duffel bag in hand, gripping the nylon straps like reins. The curtain was thin—yellowed, barely clinging to the rod. He peeled it back just an inch.

Outside, the air shimmered with heat and sirens. Flashing lights spun across the cracked walls of the Sweet Dreams Motel, painting everything in chaotic red-blue rhythm. Officers were crouched behind hoods, lined like chess pieces ready to sacrifice pawns. One had a bullhorn. Another was speaking into his shoulder mic, eyes locked on Room 9.

Then—movement.

Michael shifted the bag slightly, letting it hang down by his side. He leaned forward to get a better look at the cruiser blocking the exit.

And that's when it happened.

"GUN!"

The scream sliced the air. Came from the left—an officer half-hiding behind a black SUV. Young. Too eager. He'd caught a glimpse of the black duffel, the shoulder strap looped tight, the bag sagging in a way that *could* look like—

Pop. Pop-pop.

Then a roar.

Crack—CRACK CRACK CRACK.

Muzzle flashes lit the parking lot like strobes.

Michael dove.

Glass exploded.

Wall splintered.

The curtain disintegrated.

Bullets tore through drywall like it was wet tissue.

He hit the floor, the duffel skidding out of reach. Splinters rained from the window frame. A lamp toppled. Plaster dust filled his nose and mouth.

The air reeked of gunpowder.

He crawled backward on elbows, breath ragged, ears ringing. The duffel sat under the shattered window, one strap twitching from the impact.

Outside, someone yelled "Cease fire!" but the echoes kept bouncing off concrete like the shooting hadn't stopped.

Michael pressed himself against the bed frame.

Eyes wide.

Michael didn't think — he only reacted. The words came out of him before he even realized they were forming:

"Fuuuck youuu!" he screamed through the shards of broken glass.

His rage was answered with four more rounds ripping through the door, splinters flying. The bullets missed by inches.

He dropped lower. "That was close."

Sunlight sneaked through the holes in the battered door, dust motes dancing like ghosts in the thin beams. Jagged splinters jutted inward, casting sharp shadows across the cracked floor.

"You motherfuckers!"

"I didn't do ANYTHING!" he yelled, spit flying—rage and fear tangled in his throat like barbed wire.

The door shook again as another volley crashed through. Then—silence.

He crouched lower, breath ragged, muscles drawn tight, coiled like wire. The stench of gunpowder and hot lead thickened the air, clinging to his skin.

Outside, sirens wailed in the distance. Inside, only the sound of his pounding heart and the echo of that cursed name bouncing off the walls of his mind. The fragile thread holding his sanity stretched to the limit.

The gunfire paused.

Now he could hear them, voices murmuring just beyond the walls. Blurred. Angry. Distant.

He listened hard, trying to make sense of the mess. Trying to catch one goddamn word.

What the fuck now?

Surrender? Run? Fight? *Where?*

That relentless motherfucker brought me to this. The thought made his blood boil.

"You son of a bitch!" he screamed.

The reply came in the form of more hot lead, tearing through walls and windows at blistering speed. Glass rained down.

He pressed flat to the floor.

The room closed in.

He had no answers.

Only one question:

What the fuck do I do now?

Chapter 26: The Negotiator - Talking to Lincoln

Outside, the wind picked up, kicking dust across the Sweet Dreams Motel parking lot, where squad cars had formed a tight semi-circle of flashing blue and red. Radios crackled. Officers crouched behind open doors, rifles aimed, every breath held in coiled tension.

A black SUV rolled in slowly, deliberately—its tires whispering over gravel. The back door opened before the engine stopped.

Out stepped a tall man in a dark suit—creased but calm. Silver at the temples. Mirrored sunglasses. A yellow legal pad in one hand. His badge hung loose from a lanyard:

W. Lincoln – Federal Liaison.

One of the local sergeants approached.

"Sir, situation's unstable. Shots fired earlier. Suspect's holed up in Room 9. Possibly armed. Possibly unwell."

Lincoln adjusted his collar. Said nothing at first. Then:

"Has he made contact?"

"No, sir."

"Any demands?"

"None."

"Anyone else inside?"

"We believe he's alone."

Lincoln nodded once. Slow. Controlled. Then turned toward the motel, the air seeming to still around him. He studied the building like a man examining a puzzle box. Every detail mattered, the flickering motel sign, the bullet-riddled door, the thick silence after the chaos.

He reached into his breast pocket and pulled out a voice amplifier—nothing fancy. No headset. No vest. Just a man with a calm voice and a badge that meant too much.

He stepped forward and raised it to his lips.

"Michael Torino," he called.

His voice rolled across the lot with the slow authority of a judge reading a verdict.

"I'm not here to hurt you. I'm not the police. I'm here to talk."

He paused, just a breath, then added:

"My name is Walter Lincoln."

Inside Room 9, the name hit like a hammer to the skull.

Lincoln.

Michael stiffened, eyes blown wide, sweat cold on his back.

A twitch in his jaw. A slow pulse building in his ears like steam in a sealed pipe. Not fear this time. Not confusion.

Rage.

He stood. Stumbled once on the scattered debris, then steadied himself, staggering toward the shattered window like a man pulled by gravity.

He didn't see the cops. Didn't see the sniper scopes or hear the radios. Just one name echoing through the amplifier.

"Lincoln, you… motherfucker,"

Then louder.

"YOU MOTHERFUCKER!"

He bared his teeth, veins bulging in his neck. His voice cracked open into something guttural and raw.

"You relentless piece of shit!"

"Why?! Why ME?! You've been fucking with me for months!"

Outside, the negotiator flinched.

Inside, Michael's chest heaved.

"I see you, asshole! You hear me?! I SEE YOU!"

This is it, he thought. *This is the part where Lincoln gets closure. Where he finally takes the shot. Finally kills me.*

He stormed toward the door, then spun back, snatched the busted leg from the chair and hurled it through the window.

Something in his head buckled. A sudden, electric snap.

Then—he crumpled. Limp. Silent.

The chair leg and screams brought on another volley of bullets. Like a hailstorm of lead.

The door to Room 9 exploded inward.
Shards of drywall burst like shrapnel, the glass already gone, now only dust and echoes.

Inside, Michael didn't move.

He lay flat on the ruined carpet, face slack, eyes wide, not blinking.

No scream. No flinch.

Just... stillness.

Bullets tore overhead.

Wood splintered. A lamp behind him was ripped in two, its wires twitching.

And then —

Thwip. Clack.

Two silver canisters bounced into the room.

One skidded beneath the bed. The other rolled to a stop inches from his temple.

Pshhhhhhhhhhhhhhhhhhhh—

The hiss began. A ghostly vapor spilling out, white and cold.

Michael just stared at the ceiling.

His cheek against the stained floor, listening to the hiss like a hypnotic lullaby.

His eyes didn't water.

His chest didn't rise.

He smiled. Just barely.

Like this—this hiss, this burn in the lungs—was peace.

Another canister landed, bounced once, and spun into the closet.

Then the flashbangs came.

POP—POP—FLASH—

A high-pitched scream ripped through the air like tearing metal.

The world went white. Then gray. Then nothing but ringing.

Michael didn't blink. In fact the ringing in his ears brought on more peace somehow.

A final slam.

BOOM.

The battering ram crushed the frame and the door gave way.

Boots thundered in.

Six shadows in full gear. Gas masks. Rifles. Shoulder lights cutting through the fog.

They expected resistance.

A threat. A madman.

What they found—

was a man lying flat on his back, staring at the ceiling.

Eyes wide.

Tear tracks on both cheeks.

Lips parted in a crooked smile.

The tear gas hissed on, slow and steady, a white fog curling around him like a shroud.

One of the canisters rolled into his shoulder and stopped.

Michael didn't move.

Didn't blink.

Chapter 27: Lincoln Mental Facility

The hills were the same dull beige as the building that sat tucked between them—an expanse of concrete and faded white paint stretched like an old scar across the landscape. A chain-link fence lined the perimeter, topped with tired-looking coils of barbed wire. Not tight and gleaming like in movies. Loose. Rust-streaked. Sagging in places, as if even the fence had given up.

There was a sign near the main road, cracked and sun-bleached, its lettering once proud but now barely legible:

LINCOLN MENTAL HEALTH & REHABILITATION CENTER
— *A State Partnership Facility* —

The last few words had peeled halfway off, leaving only ghost outlines of adhesive behind.

A narrow access road wound its way up the hill, passing a security booth where no one sat, leading to the main building, a boxy two-story structure with frosted windows and a front door that hadn't been automatic since the early 2000s. Behind it sprawled the real facility: four long, low corridors stretching out like ribs, each with a flat roof and rows of reinforced doors spaced precisely apart.

Inside: white walls. But not fresh white. Faded, gray-edged white. The kind that once whispered "sterile" but now said only *forgotten*. Every surface looked like it had been cleaned thousands of times but never truly made clean.

Fluorescent lights buzzed overhead, some flickering, some dimmed to half-life. The smell was faint but constant—disinfectant, rubber gloves, and the memory of piss.

In the intake wing, two nurses moved with slow efficiency behind a wide desk. Paper forms. Plastic bins. The rhythm of routine.

Michael Torino lay strapped to a rolling gurney, unconscious or sedated—it wasn't clear. His face was turned slightly to the left, lips parted, a slow, shallow breath drawing and releasing like a wind-up toy that hadn't run out yet. His wrists were cuffed in soft restraints. His ankles too. He wore a faded blue hospital gown, open slightly in the back. His feet were bare.

A medical aide leaned over him, glancing at a clipboard. A second worker—older, chewing gum—sorted through a small clear plastic evidence pouch.

Inside:

– One battered brown leather wallet
– An Ohio driver's license
– One lottery ticket
– A motel room key labeled "SWEET DREAMS – RM 9"
– And a receipt for $42.00, cash.

The aide held up the key, looked at it for a second too long, then shrugged and dropped it into the bin.

"Jesus," he muttered. "Sweet dreams, huh?"

The other nurse didn't laugh.

From down the hallway, a buzzer sounded and a heavy door clicked open.

A heavy door swung inward with a thick, hydraulic hiss, followed by the echo of boots on linoleum.

Two security orderlies entered, uniforms mismatched in shade, keys jangling at their hips, each one built like a refrigerator with arms. One carried a clipboard, the other a walkie clipped to his shoulder crackling with distant radio chatter.

The nurse with the gum nodded toward the gurney.

"He's ready."

"Where's he going?"

"Ward C. Room twenty-eight."

"Restraints stay on?"

"For now."

They wheeled him down the corridor, past a series of locked doors labeled A, B, and finally C. Each hallway was its own sterile world. No windows. No posters. Just that same lifeless white stretching in all directions, as if color itself had been banned.

The hallway to Ward C was long, almost too long. The kind that makes footsteps sound like they're being followed. The kind that echoes even when you're alone. A fluorescent fixture overhead buzzed louder than the rest—an angry mosquito stuck in glass.

They turned left at a T-junction. A flickering EXIT sign lit up briefly as they passed.

Room 28 was near the end.

A door just like the others—reinforced, no external

handle, a single horizontal slot for observation. A faint scrape of metal as one of the orderlies keyed the lock, then pushed the door inward.

The room inside was ten feet by twelve.
Padded walls, not new. Dull gray mats bolted to the frame. A reinforced floor drain in the corner.
No bed. No toilet.
Just a single bolted bench.
And a camera dome in the ceiling corner with a red LED blinking steadily like a heartbeat.

They slid the gurney inside, transferred him to the bench with practiced efficiency, left the restraints in place, and backed out without a word.

The door clunked shut behind them.
Click. Thud.
Silence.
Michael didn't stir.

Chapter 28: The Call

The phone rang just past 9:00 a.m.

Joseph Torino was in the kitchen, halfway through a cup of coffee that had already gone lukewarm. The smell of Lucy's oatmeal lingered in the air, cinnamon and milk mingling with the low murmur of a morning talk show drifting in from the living room. Outside, Reno's sky was clear and blue, but the air carried a desert chill.

Lucy looked up from the table. "You gonna get that?"

He grabbed the phone from the wall without checking the number. "Yeah, yeah."

"Joseph Torino?"

The voice was official, clipped — the kind that came after a badge had been shown to someone.

"This is Officer Granger with the Sweetwater County Sheriff's Department. You're listed as an emergency contact for a Michael Torino?"

Joseph froze. The name, his brother's name, hit harder than it should have. Not because he hadn't expected something like this… but because, deep down, he had.

"Yes," Joseph said, standing straighter. "What's going on?"

The line crackled faintly.

"There was an incident yesterday involving your brother. He's currently in custody, he's being held for observation at a secure psychiatric facility. There was an altercation with law enforcement."

"Jesus," Joseph breathed. "Is he alright?"

"He's alive. Uninjured. Physically. He was taken in without further resistance. He's been placed under medical observation for the time being. That's all I can say right now."

Lucy had stood from the table. She mouthed, *What is it?* Joseph didn't answer.

"I… I need more than that," Joseph said. "What happened? What did he do?"

A pause on the other end.

"There was situation at a local bank. It escalated. He fled the scene. A standoff followed. It's under investigation."

Joseph gripped the edge of the counter. "A standoff?"

"Yes, sir. Your brother may be facing charges… but also, he may be placed under extended psychiatric evaluation depending on how the doctors assess him. Again, it's early."

Joseph rubbed his jaw. "Where is he now?"

"Lincoln Mental Health Facility. It's the regional secure psych unit for this area. I can give you the address."

Joseph blinked.
"What?"
"Lincoln," the officer repeated, not noticing. "Just outside the county line."

A tightness crept into Joseph's chest, barely perceptible. That name again.

He wrote it down on a grocery store receipt from the counter. His handwriting looked unfamiliar.

When the call ended, Joseph didn't speak for a moment. Just stood there.

Lucy approached slowly. "What is it?"

Joseph blinked, then looked at her. "It's Michael. He's… something happened. A standoff with the police. They've got him in some mental place out in Wyoming."

Lucy covered her mouth. "Oh my God."

Joseph stared out the kitchen window. Past the backyard. Past the low fence and the dusty hills beyond.

He didn't know what to feel.

But he knew what he had to do.

Chapter 29: The Evaluation

The hallway stretched out in front of Joseph like a corridor from some dream he couldn't wake up from, dull white, artificially lit, the color of institutional forgetting. Every twenty feet, a metal-framed chair bolted to the wall. Every ten, a closed door with a narrow vertical window, some with blinds drawn, some not.

He had just watched the detective leave, quiet apology, curt nod, then gone. The words still echoed in his mind.

"Your brother didn't write it. The FBI confirmed it this morning—handwriting doesn't match. We've reviewed footage too. He didn't do anything wrong. Not criminally, anyway."

Joseph rubbed the back of his neck, then followed a nurse to a small office tucked near the end of the corridor. The overhead lights buzzed softly. Inside, a wall-mounted clock ticked too loudly for the size of the room.

A doctor stood waiting.

Not young, not old. Her gray coat was pressed but worn thin at the elbows. Clipboard in one hand, glasses resting low on her nose. She gestured to the chair across from her desk.

"Mr. Torino."

Joseph nodded, took a seat.

The doctor glanced at the chart, then looked up. "First, I'm sorry for how your brother was brought here. It sounds like there were… several breakdowns in protocol."

Joseph's jaw tightened, but he said nothing.

She continued, professional but not cold. "Your brother has been moved to a lower-security wing since the charges were dropped. He's in Room 114 now—east corridor. He's safe. Monitored. And for the moment, stable."

"But he hasn't spoken?"

"Not yet."

"Nothing?"

"Physically, he's fine. No major injuries. Minor dehydration. Some abrasions. No signs of head trauma. But—psychologically…"

She trailed off, then sat back.

"He's not catatonic. Not in the clinical sense. But he's… disconnected. Unresponsive to external stimuli. He doesn't speak, doesn't react. He'll eat when prompted. He'll move if directed. But there's nothing behind the eyes yet."

Joseph stared at the wall behind her. His own reflection looked back at him in the framed emergency procedures poster.

"How long does something like this last?"

"There's no timetable," she said gently. "These breaks… sometimes they repair slowly, layer by layer. Other times, a sudden trigger brings clarity. And sometimes… they don't come back."

Joseph's hand tightened on the edge of the chair.

The doctor set the clipboard down. "You being here helps. Familiar faces, voices. Anchors. If there's anything left of him in there, he'll need something to come back to."

Silence filled the small office.

Finally, Joseph spoke. "Can I see him?"

"Yes. I'll walk you there."

She stood, smoothed her coat, and opened the door. Joseph followed. Back into the hallway.

Chapter 30: Room 114

The hallway stretched endlessly in both directions, long, linoleum-tiled, too bright in places and too dim in others. The walls were a dull, institutional white, the color of dried-out glue, tinged slightly yellow by years of fluorescent bulbs and stale air.

Joseph walked beside the doctor in silence, each of his footsteps echoing slightly ahead of him, as if they were being repeated by the building itself. The corridor was silent save for the soft buzzing of overhead lights and the distant, metallic squeak of a food cart somewhere deeper in the wing.

He kept his eyes forward.

Straight ahead.

The rooms flanked him on both sides, doors shut tight with narrow vertical windows. Some were covered from the inside, bedsheets or paper taped up in frantic layers. Others were bare, the glass streaked, smudged with handprints, or worse.

Now and then, he caught movement in his periphery. Shapes. Faces.

Don't look.

But his head betrayed him. It twitched, almost involuntarily. A glance.

A man pressed up against the window, motionless, staring out with eyes like saucers, his lips moving silently, endlessly, reciting something to no one.

Joseph turned his head forward again, throat tight.

More doors.

Another shape, this time curled up on the floor just inside the room, wrapped in a blanket, rocking slightly, humming something tuneless. A nurse passed and didn't stop. Joseph forced his eyes straight again.

He could feel the weight of it all. Not just the people. The lives behind those doors. But the building itself—like it had absorbed every scream, every breakdown, every second of madness and despair, and was now exhaling it through its vents.

The air tasted recycled and faintly bitter.

The doctor's steps were steady beside him. She said nothing. She didn't need to.

Another door.

Another twitch of the neck.

This time, a flickering television inside the room illuminated a man who sat inches from the screen, unmoving, transfixed, blinking only once every thirty seconds. His mouth hung slightly open, not slack, but tense, like he was waiting for something to make sense.

Joseph blinked hard. Eyes forward.

Don't look.

The corridor bent slightly, and at the end, Room 114.

The doctor paused, hand on the doorknob.

"He's inside," she said softly. "Just… take your time."

Joseph nodded once, jaw set.

She opened the door and stepped aside.

Inside, the room was silent.

Michael sat near the window, backlit by pale, dusty light, still wearing the facility-issued gown, his hands resting on his lap. His head was tilted slightly to the side, eyes open, but unfocused.

The television in the corner played something muted, nature footage. Waves crashing. Trees swaying. A deer stepping into a clearing. None of it reached him.

Joseph stepped in slowly, letting the door shut behind him with a soft *click*.

No response.

He took one more step forward, hands at his sides, just watching.

Michael didn't move.

Didn't stir.

Didn't even blink.

Joseph stood just inside the door, letting his eyes adjust to the pale light. The room smelled faintly of bleach and plastic—clean, but hollow.

Michael didn't move.

His posture was too straight to be natural, too still to be restful. He sat in the plastic chair by the window like a mannequin posed for reflection, eyes open, unfocused, trained somewhere past the glass.

Joseph took another step forward.

"Hey," he said, voice soft. "Hey, Mikey."

No flicker.

Joseph rubbed the back of his neck and exhaled through his nose.

"I talked to the detective," he said, walking slowly toward the window, toward his brother. "The one who met me out front."

He stopped a few feet away. His boots didn't make much sound on the rubber tile, but somehow the silence between each word felt loud anyway.

"He told me the FBI cleared everything," Joseph continued. "Security footage. Handwriting analysis. The whole thing. They know it wasn't you."

Nothing. Michael's hands stayed perfectly still in his lap, fingers loose, jaw slack. He was awake. Breathing. But not here.

"There's a good chance you're gonna make a full recovery," Joseph added. "That's what they said."

He waited after that. Just stood there in the space between what he said and what he hoped to see. A blink. A twitch. A single goddamn sign.

None came.

Joseph turned toward the window, then stepped over to the other chair across from Michael's, sitting down with a tired groan.

"You've always been the clean one," he said, trying to soften the edges of his voice. "Mom used to laugh when you lined up your cereal boxes by color."

Still nothing.

"I'm gonna take the Pinto back to Reno," Joseph said, looking down at his hands. "I'll fix her up. Give her a good scrub. Lucy'll help. She's already making space."

His voice dipped a little there. He looked back up at Michael.

"When you get out of here, we'll be waiting. Me. Lucy. The car too. We'll all be there."

He gave a small chuckle, but it died in his throat as he looked back into his brother's blank eyes. He tried again.

"You remember the trail up behind our old place? Where we used to race and you always made me carry your water bottle?"

Nothing.

Joseph swallowed.

His voice cracked when he spoke next.

"You're still in there, Mikey. I know you are."

He stood slowly, not wanting to rush but no longer able to sit in the weight of that silence.

As he turned toward the door, he glanced back once more.

Michael hadn't moved.

Not an inch.

The strong man's shoulders tensed, jaw locked.

He fought back the tears pressing at the corners of his eyes.

And lost.

One slid down his cheek.

He didn't wipe it away.

He just nodded once, barely perceptible, and walked out.

The door clicked shut behind him.

Michael didn't stir.

Chapter 31: The Emancipation

The overhead lights hummed with that soft institutional buzz—just loud enough to be annoying, never enough to justify complaining. Another day, another tray.

The door to Room 114 creaked open.

"Good *morning*, Mr. Torino," came the bright voice. Too bright for a place like this.

A man in light-blue scrubs stepped in, wheeling a plastic cart with a breakfast tray. He was in his forties, maybe, with a thinning ponytail and an old band tattoo peeking out from beneath his sleeve. His name tag read: **DANNY**.

He moved with an easy bounce in his step, like someone trying to keep their shoes from sinking into the muck of the job. His cheer was relentless, worn like armor against the dull white world around him.

"And how are we doing today on this *bright, sunny morning*?" he said, parking the tray beside Michael's bed. "Got something real special for you. Five-star, award-winning, silver spoon cuisine."

He peeled the plastic lid off the tray with a dramatic flourish, revealing a steaming bowl of off-white mush. "Cream of Wheat! Mmm-mmm! Just like Mom used to make, if Mom had access to industrial-grade food paste and a grudge against seasoning."

Michael didn't respond. Didn't blink. Just sat in his chair, hands in his lap, eyes forward.

Unbothered, Danny pulled up the rolling stool and grabbed a spoon.

"Let's get a little fuel in the tank, champ." He scooped up a small spoonful, lifted it to Michael's lips. "Open wide. Here comes the train."

Michael's mouth opened, barely. The mush went in. He chewed slowly.

Danny nodded, satisfied. "Attaboy."

He glanced toward the wall-mounted TV. "Let's see what's goin' on in the world today, huh? Something cheery, something light."

He grabbed the remote from the tray and flicked the TV on. A muted local commercial flashed briefly, a discount tire rotation special, before he thumbed the volume and changed the channel.

"There we go. Local news. Better than nothin'."

Onscreen, a morning anchor in too-bright makeup was finishing a story with a practiced smile.

"…officials say the Rock Springs Middle School may hire two more teachers by next semester, pending district approval…"

Danny scooped another spoonful of mush, lifted it to Michael's lips. "Big education news, huh?"

Michael chewed. Slowly. A bit of cream oozed from the corner of his mouth.

Danny didn't notice.

The anchor's expression shifted subtly as she turned to the next segment.

"And now to our top story this morning — the winning Powerball ticket, worth an estimated **One**

hundred and eighteen million dollars, still has not been claimed. Officials say the ticket was purchased at Lucky Mountain Liquor and Noodle House in Rock Springs earlier this week. So if you stopped in for dumplings and a dream—check your pockets!"

Danny chuckled to himself, oblivious. "Hell, I could use a hundred and eighteen million. I'd buy myself a new pair of knees and a cabin in Montana."

He wiped Michael's chin with a napkin and lifted another spoonful. "Come on now, can't let the mush win."

Michael chewed.

His eyes didn't move. But something behind them did.

Just a flicker.

The faintest glimmer.

As the anchor's voice droned on in the background, the corners of Michael's mouth curled — not into a grin, not yet, but a twitch. A suggestion of something stirring behind the glass.

His eyebrows lifted, just barely. The movement was minute. A tremor. But it was there.

Cream of Wheat dribbled again, unnoticed.

Danny kept babbling, spoon mid-air.

And Michael—silent, still, watching—swallowed.

—

The Pinto wagon hummed along the empty Nevada highway. Loose trim flapped in the wind. The dashboard rattled faintly with every crack in the pavement.

Joseph stared straight ahead.

The wheel steady in his hands. His face unreadable. His thoughts circling.

He didn't hear the engine.

Didn't notice the white lines zipping past.

Didn't register the radio as it crackled between stations.

Then—

A flicker.

Just as the radio signal caught—Carmina Burana drifted in. "O Fortuna…" barely audible beneath the road noise. Joseph didn't react. He just drove. His face tight, jaw clenched. Eyes flicking, unfocused. Michael's words replayed in his mind.

O-Fortuna continues in the background..........

velut luna,	*like the moon,*
statu variabilis,	*you are changeable,*
semper crescis,	*ever waxing,*
aut decrescis;	*and waning;*
vita detestabilis	*hateful life*
nunc obdurat	*first oppresses*
et tunc curat	*and then soothes*
ludo mentis aciem…	*as fancy takes it…*
dorsum nudum	*I bare my back*
fero tui sceleris.	*for the sport of your wickedness.*
Hac in hora	*So at this hour*
sine mora	*pluck the vibrating strings…*

Back in the hospital, Michael blinked slowly. The spoon paused in mid-air. The TV continued. The orderly looked down at the half-finished bowl and said softly, "You're doing good today, buddy." Michael didn't speak. But the hint of a smile lingered.

END

www.ingramcontent.com/pod-product-compliance
Lightning Source LLC
Chambersburg PA
CBHW020138120726
47903CB00007B/2305